Resistance

A Common Elements Romance

Regina Kammer

Viridium Press

Contemporary romance
by Regina Kammer

Undamaged (*Stories from the San Juan Islands*)
Modern Shorts: A Contemporary Romance Collection
Resistance: A Common Elements Romance

About the Common Elements Romance Project

Over seventy romance authors have come together to write stories that have just five things in common:
- a lightning storm
- lost keys
- a haunted house (really haunted or rumored to be)
- a stack of thick books
- a person named Max

Stories are not connected to each other in any way, nor are they in the same world. They range in length from short novellas to epic tomes. Many different romance sub-genres and heat levels are represented.

Find out more by visiting the Common Elements Romance Project website: https://commonelementsromanceproject.wordpress.com/

The Common Elements Romance Project includes *Resistance*, by Regina Kammer, an enemies-to-lovers contemporary seasoned romance novel.

Dedication

To Kotka, who persevered against all odds. I'm glad we had a bit more time with you.

CHAPTER ONE

Fort America National Park, June 2018

Perched on a rocky promontory, Kace Jaager surveyed the deeply carved river valley below. He removed his broad-brimmed hat and wiped the sweat off his brow before drinking deeply from his water canteen, ice still clanking inside the steel canister despite the heat.

The hike to the top of the eponymous feature at Fort America National Park was only five miles—if one clambered straight up. The incline was steep and the footholds treacherous, but the only other route was treading along narrow switchbacks where shale and dust crumbled under every step.

Either way, the journey took endurance, strength, and determination. Casual tourists never bothered. Which meant the trail and the plateau at the top were usually deserted.

The peace of isolation gave Kace a moment to breathe and reflect on his place in the universe. Well, okay, maybe not in a mystical sense. More like, the majestic vista of cliffs striated red and gold, the green-blue river winding through the canyon below, and the white cloud-dotted pale blue sky framing the panorama gave one perspective when the minutiae of day-to-day existence got annoying.

Shuffling papers and managing staff were the price to pay for being the National Park Service superintendent in charge of *all of this*.

He closed his eyes and inhaled the pure air, enjoying the stillness.

Until an all too familiar buzz resonated in the distance.

His lids flew open as alarm took hold, a rhythmic *whop-whop-whop* piercing the silence.

Panic battled with stupefaction leaving him momentarily rooted before blowback from a helicopter rising from the canyon slammed him to the ground. He shielded his face with his hat as the helicopter landed only thirty-five feet away.

What. The. Fuck.

A burly suit, like some Secret Service agent, jumped out of the chopper, his head bowed as he helped another passenger down.

A leggy blonde in a clingy white dress and stupidly high heels.

Kace scrambled to a crouching position and brushed dust and rocks off his uniform.

The blonde waved at the pilot. The helicopter lifted off.

With a casual elegance the blonde smoothed down the front of her dress then took a couple of steps toward the cliff's edge. The suit followed her, fawning like a sycophant. She quickly scanned the view, pointing and speaking while the suit nodded with far too much bobbing.

Kace stood and settled his hat back on his head.

She noticed. And walked toward him.

Like leggy blondes generally are, she was model gorgeous. Maybe early thirties.

She stopped before him and gave him the once over. "And you are?"

Make that late thirties. Possibly even forty. And somehow familiar.

"I should be asking you that very question, ma'am." Kace put a little more emphasis on the last word. "You're in my territory."

"*Your* territory?" Her blue eyes flashed. "This is America, right? This National Park belongs to all of us, right?"

"Yeah. But I'm the guy who runs the place."

"Oh." Her pert nose crinkled just a little. "Hence the drab uniform. Do you always dress like that?"

"Every National Park Service employee is proud to wear the green and gray. It's an honor to serve our country, *ma'am*." Emphasis with snark this time.

"How quaint. An army defending our parks."

"Protecting America's natural beauty—" it was not lost on him that this patronizing interloper was heavily made up "—and keeping visitors safe. May I see your helicopter permit?"

A faint blush dusted her cheeks before her cherry-red stained lips pursed. "I don't have one. I don't need one. I'm here on official government business."

"Oh? And may I ask what precisely that official government business might be?"

Her lips curled upward with a sinister quality. "I'm here scouting the location on behalf of Danergy Mining and Hydraulics. For our future fracturing project."

A LITTLE FLICKER OF FEAR stabbed Madison Danes' heart as Mr. Handsome Park Ranger's chiseled features twisted. His color heightened briefly to an ominous shade of crimson contrasting sharply with the shock of gray hair peeking out from under his hat.

"*You are here to do what?*" His deep voice measured every word as his bulk loomed over her.

She squared her shoulders. "I am the CEO of Danergy. I'm here scouting for our new endeavor in partnership with the federal government of the United States."

"The project has not been approved."

His certainty was disquieting. And, much to her chagrin, alluring. Plus, he was technically correct.

She raised a brow, hoping it conveyed a cool confidence she was not so sure she actually felt. "We have every assurance that the project will be approved."

"Jesus H. Christ." He gripped the brim of his hat, biceps and forearm muscles flexing beneath short sleeves. "You come here, without the proper permits, to flaunt a project that is still a pipe dream in some politician's mind?" He shoved his hat more tightly on his head. "Wait, sorry, I meant some political donor's mind."

Her heart banged against her rib cage, pumping blood to fog her brain. "That political donor happens to be my father."

Mr. Handsome Park Ranger stared, his gray-green eyes growing dark. "I thought I knew you from somewhere."

"You watch the news?"

An arrogant smirk. "Of course."

"Then that's where you know me."

"Because you're the socialite daughter of Duke Danes?"

She hated that word. *Socialite*. Hobnobbing with people was her job, not a decadent pastime. "I am the daughter of Duke Danes, yes." She met the fierceness in his gaze, almost unable to hold it. "Let's start over, shall we? I am Madison Danes, CEO of Danergy, and the daughter of the energy entrepreneur Duke Danes." She stuck out her hand.

He glanced at her outstretched arm, then speared his focus at her eyes, the icy intensity sending a chill to sear her scalp.

"And you are?" she prompted. She looked at his name tag. "Ah. Mr. Kace Jaager. And apparently the superintendent of Fort America National Park." She offered a smile.

Silence hung oppressively between them before he grabbed her hand and shook with an almost painful strength.

"I am indeed Kace Jaager—" he emphasized the pronunciation as *Jay-ger* not *Jagger* as she'd said it "—superintendent of Fort America National Park." He released her. "And I will be in my office when you are prepared to share the project plans—" he surveyed her figure then flung a glance at Max, her personal assistant who, thankfully, during times like these, doubled as her bodyguard "—and not just play games by flaunting your wealth and privilege."

He turned and headed down the hill, maneuvering along what seemed to be spectacularly treacherous paths.

Her breath hitched at how amazingly his ass filled out his khakis.

CHAPTER TWO

Kace had never hiked down Fort America's hill with such speed in his life.

Allowing fracking at America's National Parks had become a growing threat since a new administration had taken over the executive branch. However, the senators and representatives from his state and those surrounding had assured Kace such a move wouldn't happen for years, if it happened at all.

But every day offered a new political surprise. It was getting difficult to keep up. And now it looked like the mining threats were real.

Protecting America's heritage and celebrated natural beauty was no longer just his job. It was his mission.

The Fort America visitor center was buzzing with a dozen tourists browsing maps and displays, an impressive number for the summer at a relatively unknown park.

Kace hurried past the visitors to escape behind a hollow door to his private office.

Except privacy was not a concept among all his staff. About five minutes in, inexorably park ranger Paris Anderson would bounder inside to ask what was bothering him, then try to fix it.

"What's up, Kace?"

It took less than a minute before Paris was leaning her wiry frame against his door jamb, arms crossed, lips thinned.

"Close the door." He tossed his hat on the coat rack.

She raised an eyebrow and did as directed.

Kace shook his head. "You won't believe it."

"Try me."

"Remember the fracking operation across the river they've been threatening to put in since the damn election?"

Paris's eyes narrowed. "Yeeaah…"

"Looks like it's a go."

"No fucking way." Paris slicked her hand through her dark, cropped hair.

"I just met Madison Danes at the fort. Her father owns Danergy. She's the CEO. She flew in via helicopter."

"Wow. Ballsy."

"She was there to survey the area."

Paris whistled.

Kace slumped over his desk.

"Wait a minute." Grunts and the click of finger nails indicated Paris was searching her phone for something. "Holy shit, Kace. She's hot."

Yes, yes, she was. "Who?" he feigned.

"You know damn well who, you ass. Madison Danes."

Kace glanced up. "She was wearing a tight dress and heels, for chrissakes. On top of Fort fucking America. High fucking heels."

Paris laughed.

"And I should reprimand you for using such vulgar language on the job, Ms. Anderson."

She laughed harder, then plopped down in the guest chair on the other side of the desk. Her forehead crinkled as she sobered. "So it's happening then."

"Not if I can stop it."

"I'll build buzz." She furiously tapped on her smart phone. "Get environmental organizations to take this seriously."

"No, Paris. Stop," he said emphatically.

She stared at him, her hazel eyes still glazed from staring at the screen. "Sir?"

He chuckled. You could take the soldier out of the army, but you couldn't take the army out of the soldier.

And you could never drag a smart phone out of the hands of a social media maven.

"We don't have any third party evidence yet. The only people who know Madison Danes was here scouting are me and Madison Danes. And some Secret Service boy-toy she dragged along."

The sounds of a strident female voice in the visitor center filtered through the door.

One corner of Paris's mouth ticked upward. "You sure about that?"

"Fuck." He let out a heavy sigh.

"Kace, I'll slip out the back. I'll check out the scene in the center and parking lot. If there are enough people to throw suspicion off me, I'll post."

"Yeah, okay. Go." He trusted her. Paris knew what she was doing. She knew these were dangerous times. Not anywhere near as dangerous as her tour in Iraq. But increasingly worrisome.

A knock on his office door resounded the instant Paris left. "Yes?"

"Kace?" Dennis Garcia, one of the park volunteers, hissed in a low whisper. "Can I come in?"

Kace stood, opened the door, and practically dragged Dennis inside. "What's up?"

"There's a woman in the center. Nothing like our usual visitor fare." He scratched his head under his hat. "She's all dressed up for a shopping spree on Rodeo Drive, if you know what I mean."

"Yeah. And I know who she is."

"She's asking for you, or, rather, she's demanding to see you."

Kace rolled his eyes. "Can you hold her off for a few? I gotta clear my desk. She's not to be trusted."

"I got that sense about her, you know? But don't worry, you have a few minutes. Becky's got her attention for the time being, gushing over her earrings and bracelet and stuff. And you know how Becky is, she'll start telling stories and asking questions."

Dennis and his wife Becky were spending their retirement traveling the country working for the Volunteers-In-Parks program. They were as protective of their National Parks as any full-time employee. Perhaps more so. Volunteering at National Parks was their passion.

"Give me five minutes, Dennis."

The second the door was closed, Kace gathered up all paperwork on his desk then slipped it inside the bottom drawer of his standard-issue metal four-drawer filing cabinet.

He arranged the items on his desk, surveying each with regards to its utility in revealing him as a patriot, or its potential as a political liability.

And possibly an object's usefulness as an attraction—

Jeez, did he really just think that?

Yeah, he did.

He studied the framed photo in his hand, a gift from a reporter friend. A casual action shot of him in Iraq dressed in camouflage—shirt unbuttoned, sleeves rolled up—examining an artifact, his hair—back when it was brown—windswept, desert sandstone hills and army jeeps in the background. He looked a bit like a romantic archaeological adventurer in an action flick.

The kind of guy chicks would swoon over.

He placed the photo prominently on his desk. All was fair in love and war, and this was going to be an all-out war. If he had to use a sexual stratagem, so be it. At the very least, an image of him in his army days might soften the heart of a conservative business woman.

A quick rap on the door precipitated Becky's entering. "Kace—"

Ms. Danes pushed passed, her exotic perfume flaring his nostrils. He swept his reading glasses into the top drawer of his desk.

"I'm here on official business. Mr. Jaager is expecting me."

Kace waved at Becky. "It's all right." He nodded when Becky motioned as to whether to close the door.

Ms. Danes plopped her purse on an empty sliver of desk and rummaged in its depths. She produced a thumb drive. "Everything's here. Just plug and play."

He grabbed it, his fingers sliding along her slick lacquered nails, a frisson of interest nagging his crotch. He shoved the drive into his USB port and right-clicked, then clicked on "scan for viruses".

"What the hell are you doing?" Her indignant tone was matched by the deep crease between her eyes.

"Virus scan."

"Why?"

"Standard procedure for all government computers."

"But I'm working with the…" expletive suppressed by a beat "…government." The indignation was now a tad higher in pitch.

"You are working with a few politicians who have an agenda for political gain. Unfortunately, this drive is not government issue. It's from a private company. I have protocol to follow."

She sat with a huff.

"And I'd really hate to have all those cat memes I downloaded from the Internet wiped out by a virus."

She stared at him.

"That was a joke, Ms. Danes."

"Not much of one. Is that scan finished yet?"

Why was she so damned impatient? "You have somewhere to go?" *Rodeo Drive, perhaps?*

"I'm just used to a quicker pace in business transactions."

"You're working with the government now. Get used to it."

She shook her head with a grunt. Her gaze wandered over his desk. His very well-curated desk.

She picked up the photo and perused it. She looked up at him then back at the photo.

The thankfully slow anti-virus program was at sixty percent.

"Is that you?" She pointed to the photo.

"Yep."

"You look like Indiana Jones."

"I'll take that as a compliment."

"Are you an archaeologist or something?"

"The 'or something' bit. I was an archaeological field commander in Iraq during Operation Desert Storm."

The shocked silence was palpable.

"What's that you're holding?"

"A cuneiform tablet."

More silence. Afraid to admit ignorance?

He answered the unasked question. "A clay tablet inscribed with an ancient system of writing."

"You're holding it like it's a precious object."

"Well, they generally date from the third millennium BCE."

Doubt flickered across her face.

"I think the one I'm holding dates from about 2500 BCE."

"BCE?"

"Before the Common Era. Formerly known as Before Christ."

She put the photo down.

"You'd probably find cuneiform texts interesting," he continued as the virus scan leaped to ninety-seven percent. "They're all about business transactions and accounting."

"From twenty-five hundred years ago." Disdain weighed heavily on her words.

"It's your history."

"*My* history?"

"Such tablets are how the wealthy kept business records."

She grunted then stared at the computer. "No threats found. You can open it now."

Kace returned his attention to the thumb drive. He opened a new window to display the files.

"That folder." She reached over his desk to point, her salmony pink nail almost scratching the screen.

He instinctively swatted her hand away. "Just tell me the name and I'll open it."

"You don't have to be so rude."

He stared at her. "And you don't have to be so demanding."

She slumped back in her chair and crossed her arms just under her breasts, plumping them.

He returned his attention to the far less arousing computer files.

"I've opened the folder." Ominously called *Fracturing America* and containing several files.

"Open the pdf called *Fort America Project*."

Kace's gut churned as he double-clicked the document. His head spun as he read the full title: *A Preliminary Proposal for Managing Untapped Resources in the Fort America Basin.*

"Untapped resources?" Yes, he did just exclaim that out loud.

He shot her a withering look before he resumed his examination of the document, the text too blurry for comfortable reading. Kace wrenched open his desk drawer and grabbed his reading glasses, vanity be damned.

And there it was, laid out in black and white, in maps and diagrams, footnoted and indexed, the plan to violate the pristine landscape right across the river.

There was even an elevation depicting the vast scale of the endeavor. Where were they going to get the water for the hydraulic mining operation? Why by trucking it over from the rushing Refugian River along a road cutting through previously undeveloped land, using docks marring unsullied river banks.

He slid his fingers through his hair and gripped, the pulling sensation tethering him to reality, reminding him it was definitely not a dream.

Because it was, rather, a nightmare.

WATCHING MR. VIGOROUS PARK RANGER'S handsome features fade to a ghastly pallor should have spiked a sense of victory in Madison's heart.

Instead, she had to snuff out the welling disquietude before it affected her resolve.

She had one chance to prove to her father that she was every bit as badass as all the men he hired straight out of business school. And she had more to prove. She had to prove to all those men she was not accorded special privileges just because she was the daughter of Duke Danes.

Plus she was a woman. And over forty. There was so much riding on this. Too much.

Madison cleared her throat. "Do you have any questions, Mr. Jaager?"

He turned his full attention to her, shooting daggers in her direction over his reading glasses. "Questions, Ms. Danes? There are no questions, because this scheme will not be approved."

She narrowed her gaze. "And why is that?" It better not be because she was a woman, or over forty, or her father's daughter…

"Because this is a defilement of a national treasure." He stood, tore off his glasses, and began to pace behind his desk.

"Defilement? That's a strong word, Mr. Jaager." She stood, undaunted. No man was going to lord his height and strength over her.

She held the upper hand here.

"I was being polite and holding my tongue on using the other, more apt, descriptor." His words were pointed.

A chill riffled the hairs on the back of her neck. "Which is?"

His glare sliced into her. "Rape."

The chill frosted her entire body. "That sort of language is not necessary, Mr. Jaager."

He stopped and leaned across his desk. "And tearing apart America's natural beauty so you can glean a few barrels of oil and a tidy profit *is* necessary?"

"Profit is not our motivator. And it is certainly not the government's motivator."

"Ha!" His exclamation was derisive. "Oh, please do tell, what is Danergy's motivation in this venture?" He resumed his pacing, this time covering more ground.

"Our national security is at stake."

He stood before her, arms tense at his sides, fists curled, his expansive chest rising and falling in an agitated rhythm, dark gray buttons straining in their holes. "Our national security?" he scoffed.

Anger sparked, overwhelming her sense of decorum. "Didn't you say you fought in the Middle East?"

The green in his eyes flashed beneath silvering eyebrows. He took a step forward. "Yes, I served in Iraq."

His closeness was disconcerting, but she held her ground. "Then you know better than most that we need to reduce our dependency on foreign oil for our national security. We cannot rely on so volatile a region to provide so necessary a commodity."

He lurched as if he were going to strike her. Instead, his biceps flexed under his tight short sleeves. "You do not get to tell me why I served my country."

Behind the intensity of emotion ticking his face something faraway lurked in his eyes. Sorrow? Regret?

"I'm not," she said quietly. "I'm telling you why your country fought a war."

A long exhalation seemed to calm him. "I apologize. I saw war up close and personal. I would not wish such a fate on anyone." He went back to the chair behind his desk and sat. "The Gulf War was fought in part to protect a major source of jet fuel for the American military in Kuwait. I understand that completely. Not many Americans do."

"I've heard that," she said noncommittally.

"You work in—sorry, you *run* a company in the energy industry, I would be surprised if you did not know that."

His assessment of her instilled a bit of pride.

"I also understand that in the decades since that war," he continued, "the United States has taken steps to promote alternative sources of energy. Unfortunately, some administrations have thwarted such endeavors. Partly because big oil companies like your father's have politicians in their pockets."

His passion was electrifying. Too bad his passion was ill-placed.

"I am not here to discuss the merits of alternative energy, Mr. Jaager. I am here to provide you with the plans that will be a small part of America's effort toward energy independence."

His chest and shoulders slumped as he let out a sigh of resignation, scanning the computer screen, his eyes wide, his pallor replaced with an unbecoming ruddiness.

"The thumb drive and its contents are yours to peruse at your leisure. Please keep an open mind. I'm absolutely certain you will see the virtues of our project."

She offered a well-practiced smile that she did not quite feel, then grabbed her purse and marched out of the office, spine straight, head held high.

And tried to keep the image of a hunk in a form-fitting uniform out of her suddenly very active imagination.

KACE LEANED BACK in his leather recliner and stared at the dying coals glowing in the wood stove of his cabin. He'd stayed too late at the office, reading the files left by Madison Danes until he was bleary eyed, her perfume still lingering in the air, the image of her tight dress hugging her curves fracturing his already tenuous concentration, forcing him to read every document twice.

That such a gorgeous woman could be his mortal enemy was disconcerting.

But she was, and he had to proceed as such.

Paris had determined there was enough hubbub at the visitor center to offer a smokescreen to any political reporting on Ms. Dane's appearance at Fort America. In fact, apparently Madison Danes had been, at one time, married to some minor celebrity and was, for that reason alone, a minor celebrity herself worthy of surreptitious photos posted to social media by awed tourists. Once a few of them had posted photos of Ms. Danes, Paris had blasted social media from her "Rogue" Fort America accounts posing the question "What does the presence of an energy mining executive at Fort America mean?"

Of course all the other Rogue National Park accounts picked it up and for one minute on Twitter the hashtag #SaveFortAmerica was trending.

But one minute in the minds of the world wasn't going to save them. There would be a lot of work ahead, contacting environmentally-minded politicians and non-profits. And that was on top of the day-to-day management of the park, scheduling early fall school groups, and preparing the cabin for winter.

Kace let out a sigh. The road ahead was already overwhelming.

At least his adversary would be a spectacularly hot woman with a brain in her head and no qualms in showing off her curves.

Was it wrong to entertain salacious fantasies about one's opponent?

His cock didn't seem to think so and pestered him to take advantage of his relaxed state and wandering mind.

He spit on his hand and slid it under the waistband of his sweatpants to grab his erection, throbbing with need. He pumped slowly, inciting his mind to imagine the possibilities.

She'd battle with him in bed, wouldn't she? Resisting his every seductive move, his every wanton command, countering with her own demands.

She'd straddle him. He chuckled. He'd *let* her straddle him, let her think she was in control, let her glide her dripping wet cunt along his shaft, let her think she was teasing him as his prick twitched trying to slip inside.

He'd reach up to cup her ample breasts, each tit a perfect handful. He'd squeeze, then pinch her nipples between scissoring fingers, all the while rocking his crotch against her, rubbing her clit. Her eyes would glaze as she forgot herself and relinquished control for a moment. He understood. Carnal indulgences were to be savored. Heady sensations were best experienced when one surrendered.

And surrender is precisely what she would do.

Leaving her open for his attack.

The moment she would close her eyes and let out a soft moan, he would grapple her around the waist, securing her as he rolled their bodies on the bed until he was on top. She'd look up at him in surprise briefly before the shock wore off and her expression would sharpen to anger.

"You can't control me." She'd struggle deliciously.

"Oh, yes, I can. And I will."

He'd hold her arms above her head with one hand, spreading her knees open with the other, the weight of him keeping her pinned. She'd writhe in protest as he positioned himself between her legs, her exertions making him harder, making him want to fuck her all the more.

She'd be so wet he'd slide in with no effort, except to continue to hold her down. His cock would be sheathed exquisitely in her fluttering warmth, and he would stifle his growl of approval.

She should not know he was about to lose all control in her arms.

A few thrusts and his invasion would utterly subdue her. She would yield under him, her writhing sensual, her moans yearning. He'd release his hold and she would caress his arms, his shoulders, threading her fingers in his hair, tugging on the strands as her hips rocked with purpose.

He'd slam inside her, driving himself to the peak, the moment just before release buzzing with the satisfaction that he had conquered her and she had willingly surrendered.

Kace lifted his hips above the recliner as he came, pumping his semen on his t-shirt. He slumped back into the seat, then jerked forward as excitement still coursed through his body.

A minute later, after he had caught his breath, a cold sweat prickled his skin. How the hell was he going to face his worst enemy now?

CHAPTER THREE

Madison pulled her Escalade into the parking lot of the Fort America visitor center. She should have let Max drive. Well, really, in her mind, she could hear Dad telling her Maximilian should drive because of the dangerous road conditions or some stupid excuse. But the road from the Bailey, the luxury hotel outside the town of Freegate, to Fort America was at worst potholed and narrow, perhaps a bit windy and steep at points, but certainly not dangerous. And Max seemed to be doing just fine sitting in the front seat watching the scenery.

Still, Dad always said he didn't want his baby getting hurt. Except she wasn't his baby any more. Dad's latest wife, who wasn't much older than Madison, had given him a son ten years ago. So, really, her half-brother Lex was the baby.

But Dad treated Lex more like a man than he treated Madison like a grown woman.

Clinching the Fort America mining deal would be a step toward garnering his respect. And a way to step out from under his overbearing wing.

Madison needed the freedom to run a business as she saw fit, with her own goals and ideals—and staff. Some of Dad's picks were, well, a bit weird. Like Max. He was overly obsequious yet oddly useful.

She set the brake and reached for her purse, then checked her lipstick in the mirror of the sun visor.

"Ms. Danes," Max said as he grabbed his calfskin leather attaché case, "you should have let me call ahead to make an appointment. What if Mr. Jaager is unable to give you a tour? Or, what if he's not here? We'll have wasted the morning."

If she got even just a glimpse of Mr. Buff Park Ranger her morning would not have been wasted. After last night's soak in the hotel whirlpool bath and subsequent date with her vibrator, she'd fallen asleep to an image of Kace naked and in her bed, licking champagne off her body.

Which was surprising since she'd never had fantasies about food and sex—in fact, the thought of it had always seemed…messy. Yet something about the man made her want to break free of the usual and embrace the unexpected.

Or maybe it was just being free from Dad's oversight and managing this deal on her own that made her feel that way.

The visitor center was not as crowded as the day before, probably because it was only eleven in the morning. Even so, she had to feign smiles at half a dozen curious tourists who probably wondered where they'd seen her before. Her divorce had been finalized over a decade ago, and yet she still carried the stigma of being movie star Brock Branson's ex-wife.

One day she would be known simply as Madison Danes and Brock would be known as *her* ex-husband.

From behind a reception counter the perky older woman in a park ranger outfit and a long gray braid from the day before greeted her.

"I see you've returned for a visit," she said with a smile.

Madison did not want to get caught up in the woman's stories like yesterday. "I'm here to see Kace Jaager—" she glimpsed at the name tag "—Becky. Is he in?"

"I believe he just returned from making his morning rounds. Let me check."

She left the polished wood counter and disappeared down the office corridor. Madison drummed her fingernails until a tourist shot her a curious look. She flattened her palm on the cool wood, finding it difficult to resist the nervous tic.

"I told you," Max muttered way too close to her ear. "I told you we should have called ahead."

"He'll see me," she said with a confidence difficult to maintain.

A second before she was going to give up hope he emerged from his office.

Oh God. He looked better than her fantasy. And he had been naked in her fantasy.

The day before he had been sweaty and dirty and disheveled—not like that was necessarily a bad thing. But today his uniform was clean and pressed. And he wore a tie, the same dark green as his trousers. Against the light gray-green of his shirt, the effect was like an arrow pointing straight to his crotch.

His gaze swept over her, the intensity palpable even from across the room.

Her heart pounded blood to flush her face. She grabbed a map from the reception display and fanned herself.

Every step of his approach roiled her senses. She needed a distraction. She concentrated on her palm stretched on the countertop, pressing each fingertip against the wood. It worked, because suddenly he was standing—or, rather, looming, his shirt tight on his well-muscled torso—right in front of her.

"Ms. Danes, you wanted to see me?"

His voice, his deep luscious masculine voice—

"Yes, Mr. Jaager. I was wondering if you would be able to give me a tour of the highlights of Fort America?"

"A tour?" He crossed his thick arms over his burly chest.

"Yes. In my SUV, of course."

"It would have to be. Parks vehicles are all booked." His piercing glare accentuated how perfectly his gray-green eyes matched his shirt.

"And I have my bodyguard Max here with me. He can drive. If the government requires a chaperon."

A twisted smile accompanied Kace's snort. He glanced at his wristwatch, a handsome vintage piece of jewelry. Something an archaeologist-adventurer would wear.

"Okay," he said with a sigh. "You got me for two hours." He glanced at her ersatz fan. "Good, you have a map." He looked back at a park ranger, a thin young woman with severely cropped hair. "Give me a minute."

He chatted with the young woman, an older man, and Becky, gesturing with one finger pointing to each finger on the other hand as if enumerating tasks. The young woman left for a minute and returned with his hat and a canteen, handing them to him with a raised eyebrow.

And a wink.

What on earth was that about?

A bristling chill tightened her scalp. Had he said something about her to his staff?

Like he had found her attractive?

God, I wish.

"Max," Madison said quietly, "I think it best Mr. Jaager and I tour alone. There may be sensitive information about the mining project that needs to be discussed." She gave him one of her saccharine smiles. "You understand, don't you?"

Poor Max. He looked like a child left behind at a deserted gas station.

She gave him a pat on the shoulder. "I think I saw something about a shuttle bus between Fort America and the hotel?"

"Yes, Ms. Danes. I think I saw something about that as well. So I'll meet you back at the Bailey?"

"In a couple of hours."

The heat of Kace's presence behind her sent her turning around to meet a wall of chest. "I'm afraid my bodyguard has some work to do, so he won't be accompanying us."

"Fine," he said. "Let's go."

"Are you sure this is okay with the rest of your staff? They seem concerned. Especially the woman with the short hair."

Kace glanced behind him. "Paris Anderson is always concerned when the enemy is in our midst. She also served in Iraq."

"Iraq?"

"Yeah, you know the place with all the oil?"

"But she doesn't look old enough."

He scoffed. "The latest Iraq War. You do realize we've fought two wars over there."

She ignored that. "Did she also work with those—" she waved her hand "—tablets?"

"You mean cuneiform tablets?" The annoyance was palpable. "No. Communications specialist. She had to inform families back home their kid had been killed fighting an unwinnable war."

Madison shuddered. "How horrible."

Kace indicated the exit with a jerk of his chin. "Let's get on with it."

Out in the parking lot he kept half a pace behind, which was too bad as she'd hoped to get a view of his ass. She pressed her key fob twice to unlock the car. He chuckled.

"What's so funny?"

He circled around the front to the passenger side. "The color of your car matches your lipstick."

She laughed. "I was very happy when I discovered the Escalade came in Red Passion."

"Red Passion? Is that the name of your lipstick as well?"

That pesky flush heated her face again. "I don't think I can say the name of my lipstick in mixed company."

"Try me. I was in the army. I can take it."

"Come Fuck Me Crimson."

He guffawed and she quickly slid into the driver's seat, not wanting to meet his gaze. She was normally so cool and collected around men. Usually had the upper hand. But not so with Mr. Hunky Park Ranger.

He ran his hand along the center console. "Leather. Nice."

"Impressed?"

"I'd be more impressed if you drove a Tesla."

"Where the hell would I charge it?"

"At the solar array behind your Beverley Hills mansion."

She scoffed. "I mean here."

"The charging station at the Bailey. That's how they power their electric shuttle. They worked with us and the Department of the Interior on the idea." He buckled his safety belt. "I presume you are staying at the Bailey?"

"Of course. Bridal suite." She almost felt bad that some young bride was missing out on that whirlpool tub. Almost.

"Ah." He stared straight ahead. "Go left when you exit the parking lot."

"Where are you taking me?"

"You saw the view from the top of the fort down to the canyon yesterday." His voice held a censorious tone. "So you should see the view from below to the top."

There was very little conversation except for his directing her down steep inclines and along switchbacks. He seemed more reserved this morning.

"So, Mr. Jaager, did you get a chance to review the project specifications?"

"Kace, just call me Kace. And, yes, I reviewed everything."

"Good. And you must call me Madison." She glanced over at him. His face was impassive, his shoulders stiff. "Well, do you have any questions?"

He grunted. "Yeah, I do."

"Oh?"

"Pull over here. Park in that turnout."

She did so. Before she could even turn off the engine Kace was out of the car and marching up the road.

To keep up with him, she had to jog over dusty rocks and skirt sagebrush. Luckily, she'd dressed for a hike and not a cocktail party, although her athletic shoes were not as sturdy as she'd hoped. Finally, Kace stopped and looked up.

She stood at his side and followed his gaze.

It was the promontory the helicopter had landed upon yesterday. She hadn't noticed it the day before, but the feature seemed man-made, like an ancient castle. It couldn't possibly be. Still, the name implied it was.

"Why is this park called Fort America? It's not like we fought the Revolutionary War here out west."

Her weak attempt at a joke did nothing to stir Kace's placid expression as he continued to regard the jutting bluff.

He cleared his throat. "Legend has it a group of escaped slaves journeyed this far west. Native Americans helped them elude their captors by hiding them at the top of that promontory. The slaves remained there until the Native peoples assured them they were safe to leave. They then went on to freedom." He pointed, drawing a line with his finger. "If you look at that rock formation from down here, the promontory looks like a medieval fort with crenellations."

"Hence the name."

"Every summer we host a field school that does archaeological digs searching for evidence of human activity specific to the mid-nineteenth century. So far they've found a few Native American artifacts, but haven't found anything to lay credence to the story of the slaves."

"I'm surprised." She surreptitiously glanced his way. "That would have occurred only around a hundred and fifty years ago. Didn't you just say you found artifacts in Iraq that were thousands of years old?"

He looked away. Hiding some emotion? "Yep."

"So, you found those clay tablets. Surely a traveler on foot would drop something."

"Not if you were terrified of being tracked and caught. And the indigenous people would have helped them leave without a trace."

"Well, with no evidence, can we believe that story is really true?"

Kace remained silent, his chest expanding and contracting rhythmically, as if he were meditating. Or trying to keep his annoyance at bay. "Whether any of the details are true or not is inconsequential to the fact that the story is what America is all about—people struggling to remain free, to forge their own way, garnering their freedom through cooperation. It's why and how we fought the Revolution. It's why refugees and immigrants come to this country to this very day." He exhaled heavily and turned to her. "And all of this against a background of stunning natural beauty, a unique landscape found only here. In the United States of America."

His fervor was captivating. Madison cleared her throat to quell her attraction. "You mentioned you had questions about the project. What are they?"

"It's the same damn question I had yesterday."

"Which is?"

The black of his pupils dilated. "Why the fuck does the government want to destroy the beauty of this country, the history of this country, just so a few political cronies can line their pockets?"

Madison took a step back, retreating from his intensity. "And it's the same answer as yesterday. It's all for energy independence, for our national security. It's part of the administration's strategy of energy dominance."

"Then why not invest in solar power? Wind power? Tidal energy? Geothermal? In developing new green technologies we haven't even discovered yet?"

"Well, that's all very well and good, but how are Americans going to drive their cars?"

"With electric batteries recharged by solar energy."

"And how far can a car possibly go on an electric battery? Twenty miles? Twenty minutes? I live in Los Angeles. The freeways would be littered with dead cars."

"Then invest in improving the damn batteries." He balled his hands into fists. "Our wildlife and aquifers depend on the Refugian River. Fracking wastewater will trash this pristine ecosystem."

"We use a lot less chemicals in the process than you might think. And we dispose of the fluids properly."

A deep crease formed between his graying eyebrows. "In injection wells right next to those aquifers."

"We monitor all systems very carefully."

"Right. I'm sure you do." His tone suggested he thought otherwise. "Fracking does not need to be done on public land, land that should be preserved for future generations of Americans."

"Future generations of Americans will thank us for reducing our reliance on foreign energy."

He grabbed her shoulders and wrenched her to look up at the promontory. "Did you ever stop to think that your foolish pursuit of profit will have an irreparable devastating effect on this landscape? The force involved in extraction of gas and injection of wastewater will cause earthquakes in the surrounding areas." Kace lowered his face until they were practically nose to nose. "Earthquakes and contaminated water will affect everything in this vicinity, from the Bailey to our modest visitor center, to wildlife and such distinctive natural formations as the crenellations on Fort America's namesake feature."

"There is no hard evidence that fracturing causes earthquakes."

"What?" Kace croaked with a gape. "Tell that to the people of Oklahoma."

"Even if fracturing does cause tremors, they're insignificant. Nothing like the Big One. Any earthquake activity is too small to do any damage above ground."

He shook his head, mouth clenched. "That's a load of PR crap."

"No, it's industry science."

"*Industry* science?" A muscle ticked on his jaw. "Is that what you call it?"

"Look, we need energy now. What are we saving it for?"

"Jesus, are you even listening?" he growled.

"I *am* listening, but I don't think *you* are."

"Because you are spouting political nonsense." He pinched his lips together.

"What? If the natural resources are there, why not take them?"

His expression twisted as the tip of his nose hovered above her face. "Did you just say that?"

"I did, and I mean—"

His mouth covered hers. Madison struggled against him but he held her fast, wrapping his arms around her, trapping her against him, shutting her up.

Resistance was useless, and, as her body awakened to the sensuality of the barbarically physical act, resistance was becoming difficult.

How long had it been since she'd been kissed, and by a man who did not care about her fame?

Too long.

She relaxed, letting him take control, letting their mouths meld, opening further as his tongue thrust insistently. His palms spread across her back, the bulge at his crotch signified he was aroused, that he wanted her.

And the tingle in her crotch echoed those feelings.

But this was not how she had wanted this moment to happen—or, instead, how she had fantasized it would happen.

She shoved hard, kneeing him slightly between his legs. He released her, stepping back, his eyes wide as if stunned.

She stepped forward and slapped him good and hard.

HOLY FUCK. What the hell had he just done?

Kace's cheek stung from the bite of Madison's blow.

He'd never forced himself on a woman before, but, *shit*, Madison's ideas and opinions were patently wrong. He just couldn't stand listening to her spew garbage, especially when she was so damn sure of herself.

And she had all the power to put her utterly erroneous ideas into effect.

She made him feel out of control and he had to assert his control.

But, *jeez*, did he have to do it in the most monstrous way possible? His dick was still hard. And his cheek continued to burn from her understandable anger.

Crap. To add insult to injury, he was on duty. What he'd just done was tantamount to sexual assault.

He should apologize, really he should. *Shit*.

"Can you find your way back to your hotel? I'll walk back to my office."

He turned to go on his way. Madison touched his arm.

"Kace."

He flinched as his skin crawled. He couldn't look at her. And not just out of shame for what he'd done, but because in that tight t-shirt and even tighter jeans she was just too tempting.

She sighed. "This is obviously a very emotional issue for both of us. I shouldn't have asked you to show me around. I should have hired a local guide."

There was a nervous edge to her otherwise calm voice.

"Look, Kace, if, as you said, you can walk back to the center, I'll continue the tour on my own. I have GPS."

He dared meet her gaze. "It won't work. We're too remote."

"Then, I have a map. The official Fort America map." She offered a thin smile. "And a full tank of gas."

He exhaled. She wasn't acting like she was going to have him reprimanded. "All right. Be careful. The roads are not proper roads, if there is a road at all."

"Yeah. Thanks."

"And there're no lights if you're still out here at night."

"Got it."

"You have sunscreen?"

She appeared to repress a smile. "Yes."

"Water?"

"In the car refrigerator."

He chuckled as he rolled his eyes. "'Kay. Looks like you're set. I'm available for questions when you're finished."

"Thanks."

With one last look at her sexy curves, he turned and headed back to the center.

CHAPTER FOUR

Kace swallowed another gulp of water, still parched from his long walk back to the Fort America visitor center.

And still shaken by what he'd just done to a woman.

Now back at his office, he stared at the letter opened on his desk. It had arrived the day before in the late afternoon, but dated almost a week before that. The Secretary of the Interior had requested Kace and his staff be as accommodating to Ms. Madison Danes as time permitted. She was very important to the current administration.

If the Secretary ever got wind that Kace had just behaved like a dickhead, he'd strip Kace of his green and gray.

"Mail call, Superintendent Jaager."

Paris leaned against the jamb of his office doorway. "You look way too pensive, boss."

He waved her in. She tossed a stack of envelopes on his desk. They fanned out to reveal a thick one with an official U.S. Congress return address.

"Shit."

Paris snorted as she commandeered the guest chair. "What?"

He shoved the Interior's letter in her direction, then grabbed his letter opener. "Probably more bad news."

"Fuck. This is official. They want you to play nice with Ms. Tight Jeans?"

He grinned. "You noticed."

"Any hot chick wearing inappropriate clothes around here is going to get my attention."

He unfolded the sheaf inside the congressional envelope. His heart practically stopped.

"Kace? What the hell? You look like you've seen a ghost."

"I'm being summoned to appear before the Senate Committee on Energy and Natural Resources. A hearing for Senate Bill 3806. The one about developing Fort America."

"Holy shit."

"Yeah. Holy shit is right." He rifled through the pages. "There's a list of proposed questions and information I gotta be prepared to present."

"I'll do whatever I can to help. When's the hearing?"

"Two weeks."

"Jeez. They couldn't've called you?"

Kace looked at his phone, the red message light blinking dimly. "Yeah, well, they probably did."

"They're fast-tracking this."

"Looks like it."

Paris shook her head. "My Rogue contacts think the administration is using us as a test case."

"Could be. We're remote, understaffed, and not well-known." He put the pile of papers down and reached for his desk calendar. "We got a school group coming soon, don't we?"

"The Teach For America group isn't expected until later next month. How long you need to be in D.C.?"

"I hope I just need to make the one appearance." Should he also plan to meet with sympathetic politicians? His head ached from the thought.

"Well, unless Congress holds you hostage, you'll be back by then."

Jesus. This was really happening, wasn't it? Fracking? They'd obliterate Fort America. He had to stop it.

He closed his eyes as his temples throbbed.

Could any one man stop such destruction?

"Kace?"

Paris's voice shook him back to his reality. His desk, the letter, the impending doom.

She reached her hand across the desk palm up. "You okay?"

He clasped her hand then let go. He should tell her. Paris would understand. He'd gotten himself in a little too deep. He needed her to keep his back. In case something horrible happened. Like the media got wind of it.

"I kissed her."

Paris narrowed her eyes. "Who her?"

"Her. Madison. Except it was more like…well, like I forced myself."

Paris paled.

"No, it wasn't like that. Besides she was into it—"

The pallor gained an angry flush.

"Oh, Jesus. No. That's not what I meant at all." He met Paris's gaze. "I kissed Madison Danes and it was consensual. But it was a one-time deal, I swear."

"Yeah, okay. You just seem a little disturbed about it."

"I'll be fine."

She stood. "Look, I gotta go back to my cabin to do some tweeting. Becky couldn't get around to it today. The other Rogue accounts have been helping us keep up reporting what's going on here." At the door, she turned to him. "Oh, and don't worry, I won't tell anyone about how you made a pass at evil incarnate."

Kace huffed a sigh. "Jesus." Eventually word would get out about their attraction.

"Kace?"

"What?"

"Don't stay here too long. Go home, get drunk. Fort America needs you, but we don't need you at this very moment. You need to take care of yourself."

"Thanks, mom. I gotta make the rounds later. I'll just stay here and catch up on the news—"

Paris's glare was withering.

"Okay, I'll just stay here and watch porn on my government computer. What the hell do you want me to do?" He waved her out.

She laughed and exited, leaving the door open.

A sign that he really shouldn't hide in his office.

SHIT.

Madison stared at the gas gauge blaring its warning at her. She was out in the middle of butt-fuck nowhere and had run out of gas. *Brilliant.*

Dad was really to blame. He'd always told her to ignore the fuel indicator. Told her there was always more gas than the car would lead her to believe.

And now here she was—how many miles away from the hotel? Because she really had only two miles left in her gas tank. And it was getting darker and colder surprisingly quickly. Never mind that she was already hungry and tired.

There was no other choice than to spend the night in her car. Was there enough gas to run the engine to heat up the driver's seat?

Well, it really wasn't *that* cold. Best to save the little gas she had for the morning. Plus the Escalade's third row was one continuous bench and better to curl up on. *There's a sweater around here somewhere.* She turned on the light and rummaged around the floor behind her.

Ah-ha! She pulled out something soft and cuddly…and bigger than a sweater.

So that's where her pashmina wrap had gone. She smiled. *Ah yes*, the red matched the color of her car. The perfect accessory.

And now the perfect blanket.

Too bad she was all alone—

Where'd that thought come from?

Yeah, right. She knew damn well where that thought had come from. Her body had reacted quite strongly from Kace's sudden unbridled passion.

Her panties were still wet. And her mind couldn't stop replaying the moment.

But he was the last person she wanted to see right now. She'd lied and told him she had a full tank of gas. She still had a modicum of pride left.

She climbed into the third row and settled herself. Not the most comfortable bed. Maybe she'd look into getting an air mattress for those times when…

Yeah, for those times when she was out in the middle of nowhere and needed to crash for a bit. Well, now that she was managing this project, the likelihood of that happening was greater.

She stretched out. Something was missing. A pillow. She couldn't sleep without a pillow.

She climbed back to the front seat to fetch her purse. A big, soft leather tote with just a hint of padding. It would do in a pinch. Well, maybe once some of the lumpy things were dumped out.

Like her make-up bag, sunglasses case, the surfeit of pens, her keys, and her phone. Her wallet and a packet of tissues were cushiony, so they stayed inside.

She propped up her purse-pillow with the sleek leatherette Escalade owner's manual portfolio and curled up in the back seat, pulling the pashmina over her.

She probed the floor for the discarded keys. Once found, she locked the Escalade. Probably not a lot of serial killers out this way, but it was better to be safe than sorry.

Madison sighed as she put her head down and closed her eyes, willing herself to sleep.

THE DARKNESS OF NIGHT was just beginning to descend by the time Kace left his office. He should have left earlier and taken Paris's advice about going home and getting drunk. Something had compelled him to catch up on reading emails and even responding to a few.

That something was the loneliness that awaited him back at the cabin. A feeling that had been stabbing at him since his fumbled kiss with Madison.

Who was he kidding? His fumbled attempt to silence her in the most demeaning way possible.

As much as he hated what she stood for, what she believed in, she was an independent woman who knew her mind. That much needed to be respected.

Hell, every woman—every person—needed to be respected just because it was right to do so.

Fighting a dictatorship in the Middle East had not taught him that lesson—his father had—but his tour of duty had solidified it.

He flicked his headlights to high beam. The intensity of the light usually scared off wildlife, except the occasional deer so stupid they just stared. But the roads were bumpy enough to ensure one had to drive slowly, especially at night, so wildlife wasn't at risk.

It was Kace's turn to check the roads around the visitor center and just beyond. Anyone lost further afield would have to wait until morning. Generally people who ventured out to the landscape around Fort America knew to carry enough water and emergency supplies to survive a night.

He ambled along slowly, spotting nothing but the bumpy road ahead to his complete relief. Reading emails while knowing he'd have to appear before Congress had left him feeling a bit short-tempered. He'd probably snap at an innocent, lost tourist.

The road ahead was uneven, his high beams exposing rocks and potholes—

And a car stopped right in front of him.

Holy fuck.

A Red Passion Escalade.

Dread lurched in his stomach as he turned off his engine and set the brake.

Gas. She'd probably run out of gas. Nothing more than that.

But she'd told him she had a full tank.

Probably just to get rid of him after he forced himself on her.

A high-tech car like hers would've told her when the tank was low. But a woman like her would've ignored it.

A dreary chuckle rippled through him as he fished in his glove box for his flashlight, found it, then got out of his Jeep. He left his headlights on to help illuminate the scene.

He started at the front seat, shining his flashlight. Nothing.

The back windows were tinted a stupidly dark shade. From what he could tell there was nothing in the back seat.

But there was a third set of seats, something like the "way back" in his parents' old station wagon. And he would swear there was someone in that way back.

He tapped on the glass. "Madison?"

A flutter of movement. Then the back seat window opened a crack.

"Kace?"

"Madison? Is everything all right?"

A dim beam of light wavered in the seat before the parking lights flashed on the Escalade. She opened the back door and stepped out. She was wrapped in an overly large red shawl. "I ran out of gas."

He kept his smile to himself. "You can have some helicoptered in tomorrow."

She thinned her lips. "You're making fun of me."

"That was a joke and I apologize. You can't stay here, though. I can drive you back to your hotel and you can arrange to retrieve your car in the morning. Or—" he couldn't believe he was about to suggest it "—you can come home with me. My cabin is about a mile up this road."

"How far is the hotel?"

"As the crow flies, about twenty miles. But it's a lot longer on windy dirt roads."

A heavy sigh. "You got a couch?"

He chuckled. "I'll take the couch."

"All right," she said, resignation clouding her voice. "Let me grab my purse."

Once they were settled in his Jeep, he had to maneuver through some brush to skirt her SUV. About ten minutes later they were standing on his front porch.

He let her in and turned on more lights than usual.

He threw a log on the grate and lit a match, trying to calm the thumping in his chest.

A ridiculously attractive woman—a.k.a. "evil incarnate"—was in his house.

Now what?

WELL, THIS WAS NOT what she had expected. Nope. Not at all.

Mr. Studly Park Ranger lived in a cabin that could only be described as idyllic.

Or romantic.

A stone hearth—now with a fire—was the centerpiece to a wood-paneled abode that screamed bachelor-scholar. Shelves filled with books and precious items, perhaps discoveries as an archaeologist, lined one wall. A stack of thick books on a desk revealed an active scholarly interest. A worn leather recliner with a cozy blanket casually discarded across the top sat opposite the fireplace. A matching couch with decorative throw pillows faced the bank of picture windows—and TV—along the back wall.

Madison draped her pashmina wrap on the arm of the couch.

"You hungry?" Kace tossed his keys onto a brass tray by the door.

"Yeah, but I have to, um, use the restroom, actually."

He waved to a darkened hallway. "To the left. First door before you get to the office."

Presumably his bedroom was to the right.

Luckily the urge to pee distracted her from any untoward thoughts about Kace and his bedroom.

When she returned to the great room, Kace had laid out a plate of cheese and crackers and a bowl of cherry tomatoes on the Danish modern dining table next to his galley kitchen.

She helped herself to the food, only realizing as she swallowed how hungry she was.

He handed her a glass of water. She gulped it down. She hadn't realized how thirsty either.

"Thank you, Kace. I guess I didn't prepare well for my outing today." She'd only packed a bottle of water and a banana. She'd lied about her car fridge being stocked. She popped a tomato in her mouth. "These are the best tomatoes I've ever had."

"Grew them myself in my garden."

"Nice." She refilled her water at the tap then slumped against the kitchen sink. Across from her the wall was covered with certificates, plaques, and commendations. She stepped forward to scrutinize them.

Military and academic. All were issued to someone named "Kees Jaager". His father? No, not based on the dates, which ranged from the late nineteen-eighties to the nineteen-nineties.

"Who's Kees?" She pronounced it Keece.

Kace chuckled. "That's the real spelling of my name."

She lifted a brow in his direction.

"It's Dutch. But since no one can pronounce it when they see it spelled like that, I just usually spell it phonetically."

"Oh. I just assumed Kace was short for Kacey or something."

"Yeah. Most people do."

She perused the accolades. Achievements in classical studies. Service in Iraq. What else did she not know about this interesting man?

"You have a Ph.D. in archaeology?" She turned to him. "Does that mean you're Dr. Jaager?"

"Technically, yes."

"You never corrected me when I called you mister."

Amusement tugged on the corners of his mouth. "That would make me seem like a pretentious jerk, wouldn't it?"

"If I had a Ph.D., I'd flaunt it and make everyone call me Dr. Danes."

"I use the title when I represent the park in an official capacity. I really don't care if you call me mister."

She slumped against the kitchen counter. What on earth had she done in her life? Graduated with a B.A. in sociology because it was an "easy" subject at her college. Followed in her father's footsteps because that was easy, too. Married and divorced an asshat.

"Madison?" Kace's voice held concern.

"You've led an interesting life."

He stepped forward and took her now empty glass, setting it in the sink.

She looked away. He was too close.

"I'm sure you have as well."

"You don't know the half of it. None of it was worthy of an award."

"I'd give you one for being a formidable foe."

That nudged her out of her funk. She looked into his arresting gray-green eyes, the crinkles at the corners indicating amusement.

"If I weren't here, what would you be doing?"

"Tonight?" He expelled a heavy sigh. "Probably watching mindless TV."

She knitted her brows.

"It was a hard day at the office."

She laughed softly hoping it didn't reveal her nervousness. "Not what I was expecting." She was probably partly to blame for his bad day.

"Well, when the day goes without incident, I come home, cook dinner, and relax with a good book."

"Oh? What are you reading now?"

"A biography of the Roman emperor Hadrian."

"That's more like what I imagined."

He chuckled, his rigid stance relaxing momentarily before stiffening again.

He was nervous, too.

Boldness compelled her to reach for his hand and entwine her fingers in his. "Kace, thank you for saving me."

"You would have been fine until morning." His hand remained unmoving in hers. "You were just in my way going home." A slight smile played upon the corners of his mouth, fine stubble framed luscious lips.

Luscious lips that had kissed her earlier that afternoon. Kissed her without permission. Kissed her and left her wanting more.

She rubbed her thumb against the back of his hand. "We have to admit there's a strong attraction between us."

He flicked his gaze to the side, his chest raising and lowering with a shudder. "I guess."

Her lungs tightened as she tried to calm her quickening breaths. "We're both adults." Except she was as nervous as a teenager.

He seemed to be as well.

The ball was in her court, so to speak. She'd slapped him. Gentleman that he was, he probably wasn't going to make a move after that.

Gathering her courage, she lifted herself on tiptoe and brushed her lips against his.

He tensed, his hesitation melting just a little as she pressed forward, looping her hands around his neck to pull him to her.

He drew back, gripping the kitchen counter, not touching her. "Madison, you don't have to thank me for saving you in this way."

"I've already thanked you. This is different."

"Are you sure you want to do this?"

Consent. After what had happened that morning, he was asking for her clear consent.

"Yes, I do." She laid a palm against his chest, the feel of the hard muscles arousing. "Do you?"

"My mind is at war with my body right now."

She grinned as she plucked free a button on his shirt. "Who's winning?" Another button.

"I would say you are."

She stopped. "I think we should put aside our political differences for one night and enjoy ourselves. Maybe that's all we need."

"So, a one night stand?"

"God, that sounds horrible, doesn't it?" She sucked in air. "Look, it's been a while for me—" a few years actually "—so maybe I just need to get Mr. Hunky Park Ranger out of my system."

"Is that what you call me?" He laughed. "I guess fair is fair."

"Why, what do you call me?"

"Ms. Tight Jeans. And it wasn't me it was Paris."

Shit.

"She's into chicks and noticed everything I noticed. She just said it out loud. She's like that."

"Oh." *Whew.* Last thing Madison wanted was a jealous lover to spread rumors to the press.

He palmed her hips, his fingers pressing into her butt, the warmth of his touch firing off every erogenous nerve in her body. He leaned in, slowly drawing the tip of his nose down her neck from her ear to her collar. Arousal flashed through her, pebbling her nipples, tingling her cunt.

"One night with Ms. Tight Jeans sounds like fun." His words fell hot against her already flushed skin. She was going to melt into a puddle at any moment.

He retraced the path on her neck, this time with the wet tip of his tongue, accompanied by a scrape of stubble.

She sagged from the sensual thrill. Luckily the counter was there to catch her.

He grabbed the hem of her t-shirt and pulled it over her head. With a raised brow and a bite of his lower lip, he gazed at her barely-there lace bra.

"I know it's not typical hiking gear."

He laughed, then unhooked the back, slid it off, and dropped it on the counter.

The tips of her breasts puckered with excitement and the chill of nudity.

"Beautiful," he murmured, then took a yearning nipple in his mouth.

Pleasure jolted her then rippled like a wave, her body followed the sensation, undulating and arching.

Kace tugged at the waistband of her jeans, wasting no time in his effort to undress her, his focus and zeal leaving her dazed and flustered.

She needed to get a grip. She wanted to see him, too. Wanted to see those burly muscles straining his clothes.

Her fingers fumbled as she tried to untuck and unbutton his work shirt while he continued to suck and lick her taut areola, the one on the right side now. Finally she was able to tug off the gray button-down to reveal his white v-neck undershirt.

Snatching his hands away, she thwarted his determined attempt at taking off her jeans, which were, admittedly, a bit tight. She grasped the hem of his t-shirt and pulled it up and off.

Before her was a sculpted hunk, pectorals furred with brown hair flecked with gray. Her admiration was cut short as he bent down to remove her shoes, mortification that they were pink and orange and barely worn spiking through her. He made no comment as he finally peeled her jeans down to her ankles. She held on to him as she stepped out of each tight ankle, while he held her socks on.

The shoulder she gripped sported a scar silvered with age. She traced the line that marred his perfect body. A chill of realization crept over her.

"From the war?"

He stood. "Bullet grazed me. Luckily that was all." Mischievousness flickered across his expression. With both hands on her waist, he lifted her onto the cool stone counter, then looped his thumbs on either side of her panties and pulled them off, dropping them next to the bra on his counter.

"Now, didn't you say something about how it's been a while?" He grabbed her knees and spread her open to his wolfish gaze.

He cupped her butt cheeks and pulled her to the edge of the counter. He stooped, his face right between her legs. Her cunt flexed in anticipation.

Kace leaned in and pressed his mouth to her.

A glorious shockwave of rapture tore through her as his lips and tongue took her on a journey of ecstasy, the grunts of his enthusiasm mingling with her gasps and moans. She tried to hold on to the counter, to the cabinets, anything stable as he jostled her in his abandon, lifting her at times with the tips of his fingers, his nails biting into the flesh of her butt. She threaded her fingers through his hair, pulling as each mini-orgasm burst, her actions seemingly egging him on to take her all the way.

His relentless sucking on her clit sent her teetering over the edge. The spark of orgasm smoldered in her belly, igniting too-long dormant desires, then flashed through her core, exploding her senses.

Amazing. Simply amazing. Exhilarated exhaustion weakened her, as if she had just run a mile.

He rose, standing between her legs, and licked his lips.

She draped her arms around his brawny shoulders. "That was magnificent," she sputtered, still coming down from her orgiastic high.

"Thank you," he answered with a devilish grin.

Suddenly, he scooped her up, the hair of one forearm tickling the backs of her calves, while the palm of his other hand cupped her breast. Like a hero in a Highlander romance, he carried her to the small hallway, turned to the right, to his bedroom. He laid her gently on his bed, as if she were precious.

He raised a brow as he unbuckled his belt.

"My turn."

*****

SOMETHING ABOUT MADISON Danes brought out the he-man instinct Kace had worked all his adult life to bury deep within. The army had taught him discipline, had taught him when it was the right time to be a soldier or a diplomat or at ease.

And right now, in front of one of the hottest woman he'd ever seen, he was going full-on peacocking macho stud.

Like a stripper he put on a show of sliding off his belt as she stared dumbstruck, alternating biting her lower lip or a pink-polished fingernail, hugging her legs against her naked body.

He unbuttoned his waistband drawing attention to the bulge at his crotch. Her eyes widened.

Boots had to come off first. He suggestively propped a foot on his dresser and unlaced a hiking boot, then switched feet and did the same with the other. He toed them off slowly, one at a time, never taking his eyes off her, even when he bent down to pull off his socks.

She swallowed as he unzipped his fly.

Her melodic whimper filled the air when he took it all off, pants and briefs. He posed before her, hands on hips, giving his pelvis a little jerk to get his balls swinging.

Was that fear in her eyes? Or excitement?

Did it matter?

Shit, yeah, it did. But the Neanderthal inside was egging him on regardless.

He climbed onto the bed, jostling the mattress. She released her grip on herself as she gained purchase. Now she was disarmed, he urged her to unfold fully. She relaxed as she lay back, letting him stretch over her. His erection nestled against the softness of her belly, the wetness between her legs warm against his thighs. He looked deep in her eyes, the pupils swelled to make her blue eyes black.

He captured her mouth with his, thrusting his tongue deep inside, a prelude to what awaited her. She arched under him, her bounty of tits pressing against his chest, her legs wrapping around his hips.

She was ready.

He rolled off to dig around in the top drawer of his nightstand. Yes, he did have condoms, even if he rarely got the chance to use them. He grabbed one.

She stilled his hand.

"Let me." Her voice held that gravelly edge that was so profoundly sexy.

He rolled onto his back. "Really? You want to do the honors?"

She laughed. "Sure." She slid down his body, kissing and nipping along the way, each nibble sending an electrifying shiver through him. She stopped over his crotch, her breath humid against his cock.

He yelped in shock when she took him into her mouth.

Oh god oh god oh god oh god… She knew exactly what she was doing to him. And what she was doing was, oh, so very good.

She set him free with a *pop*, then tore open the wrapper and unrolled the condom over him excruciatingly slowly, her erotic *ministrations* making him harder by the second.

She admired her handiwork. "Impressive."

"Thank you." He twitched his cock.

She laughed a natural laugh, like a woman so utterly sure of what she wanted. And what she wanted at that moment seemed to be him.

He cupped her cheek. "You want to be on top?"

"Uh, oh. Is that what you want?"

"It's what I imagined you'd want."

She crawled cat-like over him. "Which means you imagined what I'd be like in bed."

"Don't tell me it didn't cross your mind what I'd be like."

There was that laugh again. "I think I mostly just thought of you naked."

"And?"

Her lower lip disappeared between her teeth for a moment. "Oh, you're better than I imagined." She raised a brow. "Like I said, impressive."

She straddled him, hovering a moment while she looked him in the eye, naughtiness playing on her face. She gripped his shaft for guidance and lowered herself languidly, taking him inch by frustrating inch.

At the hilt, she tried to take him even further, then squeezed with an incredible force.

The ensuing wave of bliss numbed him to whatever expletives he mumbled.

She commenced her upward motion, maintaining that exquisite pressure all the way to his tip. Then she relaxed her muscles and slid down again. She knew exactly what she was doing.

And what she was doing was controlling his pleasure.

Somehow that was freeing. He relaxed under her, letting her take what she wanted from him.

Because inside the bedroom, his physical strength meant he held the power. He gave her control.

Outside the bedroom, he would not be so generous.

He grasped her hands as she pistoned wildly, losing herself in a sensual frenzy. His balls tightened, his need for release imminent, his desire to see her come holding him at the precipice.

Letting go with one hand, he pressed his thumb against her clit, his other hand holding her steady as she bucked from the sensation. Her jaw slackened, her head fell back, her moans filled the air.

She clenched hard around him, howling her orgasm. He let loose, bucking his hips against her, relishing the flutter of her cunt as she panted erratically, slowly settling down until she slumped over him.

"That was good, Kace." Her heart pounded against his chest. "Really good. I needed that."

"Yeah," he groaned. He'd needed it, too.

CHAPTER FIVE

Madison opened her eyes, a split second of panic skipping over her before she realized where she was.

In bed with the enemy.

Except the enemy wasn't at her side. The sound of water rushing through pipes indicated he was taking a shower.

She scanned the room for a mirror. Not many men had them. Kace did, though. An antiquey one in a polished wood frame on top of his dresser. Probably because he wore a tie to work.

Her hair needed a bit of taming. Perhaps a comb. And her makeup was all but gone. She padded off to the great room to retrieve her purse.

An expanse of windows, dark during the night before, displayed an astonishing sight.

Morning sunlight spilled over a rocky landscape, a bit of brush and a scattering of trees throwing gray shadows against the golden ground. Behind it all was a canvas of cerulean blue, pale along the horizon, a deeper shade as it approached heaven.

And she utterly nude before it all. Okay, except for her socks.

Her red pashmina wrap lay on the couch, but Kace's shirt hung invitingly over a kitchen chair. All their clothes from the night before had been picked up off the floor or counter and draped over the backs of the dining set. Kace must have done that sometime in the middle of the night.

How sweet.

Madison slipped on his shirt, then grabbed her purse and dug in. *Shit*. No hairbrush, no lipstick, no makeup.

No anything.

A shiver ran up her spine. She frantically searched the pockets again.

No keys.

Damn. In her mind's eye she saw them on the floor of her Escalade.

Jeez. If her Escalade was even still in the middle of nowhere. Of course it was. No gas. Except car thieves could be rather persistent when they wanted something badly.

"What're you doing?"

She started at the sound of Kace's voice. He leaned against the jamb of the hall doorway wearing nothing but a towel, his chest hair in damp curls plastered against his magnificent physique. He sauntered toward her.

Her heart pumped blood to her sex. She still wanted him. *This is bad*. Very bad.

"Searching for my lipstick."

He dragged a thumb across her lips. "You don't need that, you know."

She stilled his hand. "I want it."

"Do you know how beautiful you are?"

Heat rose to flush her face. At least that would bring color to her washed-out morning complexion. "Thank you."

"A natural beauty like you shouldn't hide behind such nonsense."

"A woman like me enjoys all that nonsense, as you put it. I *love* wearing designer clothes and I *want* to wear eyeshadow and nail polish." She waggled her salmon-pink nails at him. "It's fun."

"I say you look pretty damn good standing there in my government shirt and no lipstick. You don't need to impress a guy like me." He gave her butt a little swat on his way to the kitchen.

"I'm not trying to. I do it all for me." That was only partly true. She loved wearing tailored suits and make-up, but sometimes yoga pants and a ponytail fit her mood.

"You want coffee?" He looked up from pouring beans into the hopper of his coffeemaker.

"Yes, please." She watched, riveted, as he made coffee while practically naked, the towel barely clinging to the curve of his butt.

She needed a distraction. Her phone.

Probably right next to her lipstick in her car. Hope compelled her to dig inside her purse.

Glee almost burst into laughter when she found it tucked inside a pocket. Right. She'd used it as a flashlight when Kace found her. So she could unlock her car, then promptly drop her keys on the floor mat.

Ugh.

Well, she knew where her priorities lay. Her phone, not her lipstick. Or keys.

She turned it on. A pretty respectable twenty-three percent charge remained. But no messages.

Odd.

"You do cream or sugar?"

Kace's voice brought her back to the moment. "Black's fine. Thanks."

He handed her a mug.

"So, do you have cell service out here?"

He chuckled. "Not really. It's mostly Wi-Fi." His gaze flicked to the phone in her hand. "Just navigate to your Wi-Fi settings and I'll put in the password."

She did as instructed, then handed him her phone.

How she wished she could take a photo of Mr. Handsome Park Ranger nakedly setting up her mobile connection.

"Try it." He handed the phone back to her. "Should work."

Every notification imaginable popped up across the top. Texts, email, phone calls, social media. She opened her texts. Max was frantically looking for her. Poor guy.

Emails were from Dad, her foundation…damn wasn't there some paperwork due?

"Oh, jeez," she said under her breath.

"Gotta check out your Texas oilfields by helicopter today?"

She responded with a scowl.

Kace took a swallow of coffee. "So, what is it you do, anyway? If I'm allowed to know, that is."

"Well, I'm CEO, so lots of meetings," she sighed. She sipped her coffee, a surprisingly good blend for butt-fuck nowhere. "I manage the L.A. office and lobbying in Washington, D.C. That's why I'm here, since Fort America is reasonably close to L.A."

"And is a political football."

"Not really so much anymore with this administration."

"Yeah. That's the problem isn't it?" Kace refilled his cup and leaned against the counter, his expression sullen. "Why L.A.?"

"I've lived there for a really long time—" with a jackass of a husband, "—so we set up a corporate office in downtown. Dad stays in Texas. He loves to visit the oil fields. Makes him feel like a cowboy."

Her phone buzzed again. A text from Max. "Shit. I gotta get back."

"Bodyguard looking for you?"

"Yeah. And my foundation."

"You have a foundation?"

She eyed him quizzically. He really had no idea who she was, did he? "Yes," she said. "The Dama Energy Foundation."

"Huh. I guess all rich people have foundations." He finished his coffee and put his mug in the sink.

"It's how we launder our vast sums of money."

He paused a beat too long. "That's a joke, right?"

She shook her head in incredulity as a grin spread across her face. "It's a non-profit to help women achieve success in energy and engineering-related careers."

"Oh. Not what I was expecting."

"Why?"

"Sounds kinda…well, feminist."

"But I *am* a feminist."

"A feminist? In come-fuck-me lipstick and high heels?"

She hoped her glare stung. "So I like to wear fancy shoes and bright red lipstick. A celebration of femininity is not counter to feminism. And you don't get to tell me how to be a feminist."

Surprise crinkled his expression. "Someone got woke."

"You have to be to stay relevant these days."

"Not the kind of thing I expect a Republican to say."

"No? Well, maybe get to know some."

"I thought I was," he murmured, a sexy gleam in his eye.

She scowled. "Look, sexism, and any kind of discrimination, is simply bad for business. I just wish more of my colleagues would understand that." She placed her hands on the towel at his hips. "And as much as I'd love to get to know you more and tell you all about myself, I need to get back to my hotel, get gas, and get my car."

Disappointment clouded his expression. "Yeah. Right. I gotta get dressed."

He didn't move.

"So," she said. "Go get dressed."

"That's my shirt."

She pulled it off and handed it to him, his disappointment morphing into something akin to lust as his gaze raked across her naked chest.

"Go." She pointed to his bedroom.

Ten minutes later, after having dressed in the kitchen where all her clothes had been carefully hung, she and Kace left the cozy cabin.

Daylight revealed how cute the structure was. Barely weathered wood and large windows with a modern, outdoorsy feel, but with all the amenities like a satellite dish—

And solar panels.

Of course.

"You don't have power strung out here, do you?"

He narrowed his eyes then followed the direction of her nod. "The cabin is off the grid. With the climate here solar is pretty reliable, as is the wind turbine. I have a system of batteries, plus backup generators to run essentials like the well pump and refrigerator in an emergency. My oven and stove are propane. The well water is supplemented by a rain water catchment system, plus gray water recycling. It's a Park Service experiment to see if we can create sustainable infrastructure for remote sites like Fort America."

"And how's that experiment working?" A morning chill still lingered in the air. She pulled the pashmina more tightly around her.

"Quite well. We were thinking about geothermal, but," he frowned, "the political climate is not amenable at the moment."

His frosty delivery sent a chill to creep up the back of her neck. "But you have TV."

"People can still be connected and live with less impact on the earth. I'm not a hermit living a disconnected life. I do have Wi-Fi and TV."

"And the rest of the staff?"

"Theirs are still old-school cabins on the grid, closer to the visitor center. I volunteered to be the guinea pig. There's a lot of energy monitoring and data gathering that comes with the experiment. Almost like having a second job."

He opened the passenger door to his Jeep, the gallant gesture reminding her of his rescue the night before. Last night's sordid assignation, and this morning's quasi-bickering had eclipsed his previous gentlemanly behavior.

She climbed in and settled herself as he started the engine.

"Kace, I can't find my keys. I think I might have dropped them on the floor of my car."

"So you locked yourself out?"

"No. It isn't locked. But the keys are inside. Anyone could've taken it."

He skillfully maneuvered the Jeep on the bumpy road, before shooting her a glance. "You're serious, aren't you?"

"Well, yeah."

A chuckle rumbled in his throat. "I guarantee you your car will be exactly where you left it."

The landscape dotted with dusty green brush and red-gold boulders was deserted. Okay, yeah. From the looks of the place, Kace was probably right.

He drew in his lips, obviously trying not to smile. "There might be a family of rabbits under the chassis. I'll check."

"Good." If he was teasing her, she'd give it right back. "When we stop at my car I can pick up my lipstick."

He shook his head with a low chuckle and continued down the road.

KACE PROPPED HIS elbows on his desk letting his head fall into his hands. He blew out a long sigh.

He'd given her his cell number, asked her to text him when she was back at the hotel and safe. Had grabbed breakfast at a diner in Freegate so he'd be nearby in case she needed his help. But Madison hadn't contacted him yet, and he was starting to worry. She was just so unprepared and out of place in this environment.

She'd assured him Max would take care of retrieving her car. She'd had it all figured out.

Besides, he should not be worrying about the person whose sole purpose was to destroy life as he knew it, not to mention his livelihood.

And, yet, he was, because he couldn't get her out of his mind. Why the hell did he decide to wear yesterday's shirt, the same goddamn shirt with the faint trace of her perfume clinging to it?

Because that's what the damn caveman within had told him to do.

Fuck. Paris would figure it out in less than a second.

A knock on the door. *Double fuck.*

"Kace?" Paris's voice held concern.

"Yeah. Come in."

She entered and closed the door behind her, staring at him, every movement laden with scrutiny. She sat. "Something's bothering you."

"Not looking forward to D.C."

Her eyes narrowed as she crossed her arms. "Nope, that's not it."

Shit.

"You slept with her."

Was this one of those times when he had to play the boss card and tell her about inappropriate conversation?

"Kace, what the fuck?"

And now the subordinate was scolding the supervisor. In this case she was well within her rights.

"Madison Danes isn't some transitory tourist you'll probably never see again."

One night stands with tourists were pretty much all he ever got with this job.

"She's the fucking enemy—"

And the best lay he'd had in probably twenty-five years.

"And she's going to be at that Senate committee hearing all smug and mocking."

To compound the insult, the nagging feeling of wanting to see—or rather fuck—Madison again was driving him crazy.

His cell phone buzzed. *Her.* "Paris I have to take this."

"Okay." Paris stood. "Look, boss, just don't lose your heart. You'll never get it back."

Oops.

CHAPTER SIX

Washington, D.C., two weeks later

Whenever Madison met up with Dad in a big city, he'd always find the most old-fashioned restaurant for their meetings. Sammy's Tavern in the heart of Capitol Hill oozed nostalgia, like something out of the fifties, where the lighting was dim and the red leatherette booths made it even dimmer. Because the decor harked back to an era when men were captains of industry and women stood dutifully at their sides, a politically conservative vibe reigned supreme.

Luckily Madison had the *maître d'* to guide her through the labyrinthine crush of tables, their way lighted almost solely by the dim glow of candles in red glass votive holders. Dad's booth was tucked far away in the back.

Dad stood when he saw her and emerged from the tufted banquette, straightening his tie.

"Maddie." He held his arms wide as if about to hug her. But Dad never hugged her straight on, like a proper hug, a hug a father would give a daughter. It was always more like an exuberant version of an arm around the shoulders. Something he did with all his female business associates. With the men he just shook their hands.

"Hi Dad."

Dad placed a hand on her shoulder then stood back to give her the once over. "Maddie. How lovely you look. All dressed up." He winked, as if she were dressed up for a date and he approved.

She smiled while inwardly rolling her eyes. She had chosen a simple but classic Chanel suit for her meetings with senators and representatives, with a sleeveless top underneath for the humid summer weather. So, fashionable but with an eye toward modesty, professionalism, and practicality. Definitely not date attire.

"Thank you, father of mine."

He gestured to the booth and she scooted in to sit along the leatherette cooled by air conditioning. He sat opposite.

"How was the trip out to the middle of nowhere?"

She laughed at his apt description of Fort America. "Very enlightening."

Dad waved at the waiter. She'd be having whatever he'd prearranged for her. Probably a salad when she could really go for a bowl of linguine in clam sauce.

"What can we expect from the locals? You think there'll be opposition? We really can't put up with shenanigans if we're to proceed on time."

"There really aren't any locals as such." Except Kace. But he was a government employee. He had to do what he was told. "Just National Park employees."

"They'll object. They always object. As if they owned the land."

Well, they *were* charged with being stewards of America's open spaces and natural beauty, so…

"What about nearby towns?" Dad indicated to the waiter that the shallow bowl of pasta marinara was for him.

"Freegate is closest. Typical small town with tourist amenities, you know, like a small grocery store, gas station, camping supplies. Some touristy shops." She sipped her water, wishing it were wine. "I've got an offer on some cheap property there. For when I have to spend time overseeing the project."

Her salad arrived. Dressing on the side. At least it was ranch. A warm and fragrant basket of garlic bread followed.

"Good, good," he said, digging into his food. "We want to avoid any confrontation. It's why we picked the site. Far from large groups of organized protesters."

Although these days, protesters didn't seem to mind spending money on airfare. "There are plenty of campsites at Fort America, Dad. We should be prepared."

"I think we can handle a bunch of hippies."

Madison grabbed a chunk of garlic bread and sunk her teeth into it. She chewed as she gathered her thoughts. "There's a really nice luxury hotel and spa just outside of town. For those not up to camping. There were a lot of tourists."

"Hmm," Dad said with his mouth full. "A small exhibit in the lobby about our need to ensure energy security should do the trick."

Probably not for the kind of intrepid, environmentally conscious tourist she saw on her visit. She dribbled dressing on her salad.

"What's the source of drinking water?"

"A couple old reservoirs and the Refugian River."

"Aquifers?"

"Yes, with several residential wells tapping into it."

Dad swiped his linen napkin at the corners of his mouth. "Good work, Maddie."

"Thanks, Dad. I'm meeting with Senators Wade and Young this afternoon. I'll let them know we might have more backlash than anticipated."

"Don't worry your pretty little head about it, Maddie. I've already spoken with Randall and Greg."

Madison stopped chewing. She swallowed. "You did what?"

"We had lunch yesterday. Everything's been taken care of." Dad ate a mouthful of pasta.

What the fuck? She held her cool. "Dad, this is my project. I need to meet with them directly."

"Maddie," Dad began with a wave of his fork, "sometimes deals are best done by men who have a long history together."

She dumped the rest of the ranch dressing on her salad, then stabbed at the lettuce, eying her water glass, now wishing it was a ginormous martini. "Dad, we have discussed this before. How can I gain a decent foothold in this industry and appreciate all of its nuances if you do not let me run my own show?"

"I apologize, dear. You go ahead and meet with Senators Wade and Young as much as you like."

The crunch of lettuce was overly loud, drowning out her indignation. "I will, Dad. I very much intend to keep my meeting this afternoon."

"Good. Any other news from your excursion?"

No. Nope. Nothing. Nada. She would absolutely not tell him anything else if he was going to go behind her back like that. "Fort America is a pretty spectacular place. I'm looking forward to spending time there."

Madison concentrated on eating and listening to Dad's chit-chat and gossip, her mood not conducive to productive father-daughter conversation. The highlight of the lunch was a *paparazzo* asking to snap a photo of the two of them.

She just hoped she didn't have lettuce in her teeth.

Dad had his cronies and she had hers. Some of hers were senators and representatives, some business people. Most of them were women. They needed to know that if a woman was going to head up this mining operation, that particular woman would be making the decisions and swinging the deals.

She'd meet with Senators Wade and Young then make some calls. She'd organize meetings with whatever female legislators she could find.

KACE STEPPED INTO the lobby of the Federalist Hotel, closing the gate of the hundred-year-old elevator behind him. The building itself was even older, the former home of an actual Federalist, one Barnabas Fouch, an obscure Founding Father. The hotel staff claimed his ghost still roamed the hallways, trying to protect his townhouse from marauding British troops on their way to torch the Capitol in 1814. Most probably Fouch was simply trying to find his way through centuries of renovations and looking for some way to beat the oppressive summer heat.

For the umpteenth time, Kace made sure his briefcase held everything he would need during meetings with the senators from the states Fort America spanned across. A printout of his opening remarks for the hearing, a blank yellow legal pad, extra pens, business cards, his wallet, and phone, were all tucked away in the leather case he'd bought in France decades ago but rarely had a chance to use. He crammed his wallet into his front jeans pocket.

Behind him, the elevator doors clanged open.

"Kace? Is that you?"

The familiar, and very welcome voice of Bettina Yeager, his Park Service colleague from San Francisco, immediately calmed his nerves.

"Bett, lovely to see you." He gave her a warm hug.

"Tell me, what's my brother from another mother doing in D.C.?" She looked him up and down. "And in civvies?"

Kace laughed. Once, at a history conference, Bettina had joked that given the similarities of their last names they were probably descended from the same Viking raiders. That she was black and he was white spoke volumes about the posited theory.

"I should ask you the very same thing," he said. She was wearing street clothes herself. "I understand it takes a lot to drag you away from San Francisco."

"My staff is the best in the National Park Service. They can handle a few days without me."

"And my staff is constantly telling me I need to get out more."

Bettina laughed. "I'm here doing research at the National Archives. Gotta get all my groundwork done and copies made before I retire."

"Retire? What? When?"

"I was planning on two years from now. But it may have to be earlier." Bettina glanced around, a hint of suspicion curling the line of her mouth. "I can't stand the stress of what's going on in the Service right now," she said in a hushed tone, "and what's in store for the Department of the Interior."

"I get that." Kace grunted in agreement.

She looped her arm in his and led him to the small waiting area. She looked around again.

"I don't think anyone's listening, Bett. Except the ghost."

"I imagine Mr. Fouch is appalled at the state of our union these days." She sat on a worn velvet settee.

He joined her and gave a brief hug around her slumped shoulders.

"The new higher ups are expecting personal loyalty to their political agenda, not experience and good park management skills. With all the reassignments and the accusations that some of us are not loyal Americans…" Bettina shook her head. "I just gotta get out."

Kace knew all too well about the shake-ups. He'd counted on Fort America being under the radar and his position not being affected. But Madison Danes showing up on his doorstep was proof of the new political landscape. "I can't believe you're anywhere near retirement age, Bett."

She framed her face with her hands and offered a silly smile. "Melanin softens the wrinkles and hides the stress. It's the one benefit of being African-American these days. And knowing how to cover the gray."

He chuckled. "What's your research?"

"Blacks in the Pacific maritime industries. My intention is to write a book in my retirement. The last few days in the Archives have been quite productive. You here doing research?"

"No. Senate hearing on the economic future of Fort America."

Her expression soured. "Don't tell me it's that fracking shit I keep hearing about?"

"Yep. Now known as Senate Bill 3806."

"Dang. Then it's real."

"Yeah. The Rogues think we're a test case. To see what the backlash is so those higher-ups can prepare for future deals."

Bettina shook her head with exasperation. "I'll do what I can, you know I will."

"I know, but I fear it's a done deal." He'd braced himself for hearing exactly that at his meetings today. "Hey, what about dinner tonight?"

"I'd love to, but I can't. I'm flying home this evening." She patted his leg. "You heading to the Mall?"

He nodded.

"Let's share a cab."

On their cab ride, Bettina recounted all sorts of political horror stories from other National Parks—along with stories of triumph—riling and soothing him in ways only an experienced government veteran could. He rode with her all the way to the National Archives. One last hug goodbye energized him to fight the good fight.

A skip in his step, he walked to the Senate office complex, taking a detour past the front of the Capitol building. His life had been in service to the United States, and the neoclassical edifice was a powerful symbol of the American people, their democracy, and their freedom. He disliked the hustle and bustle of D.C., having to dodge dazed tour groups and harried office workers. But, *damn*, if the sight of the Capitol dome didn't fill him with pride and patriotism.

Curiosity made him slow his pace as he approached a small gathering on the marble steps. There was something familiar about the woman who was the center of all the attention—

Every hair on his head stood on end.

Perfect, poised, and professional, Madison Danes was talking to what looked like a group of reporters while a photographer took pictures.

She was gorgeous in a pink tweedy suit with a Sixties flare, looking like a sexy, blond Jackie Kennedy. Arousal in his crotch reminded him he was in public. He really should not be staring.

In mid-sentence, she met his gaze.

She paled. Then blushed.

He picked up his pace and continued on his way, holding his briefcase in front of him, hoping to God none of the reporters had caught that brief moment of indiscretion.

"ARE YOU PLANNING ON expanding operations beyond Fort America, Ms. Danes? Like at other sites on the Colorado Plateau?"

Madison forced her attention back to the reporter from the *Examiner*, thankful he did not notice she'd been distracted.

And, *good God*, was it a distraction.

Kace had been wearing jeans, the blue denim hugging every curve of his butt. A sky-blue polo shirt—not the drab button-down of his uniform—clung to his torso, accentuating his brawny shoulders and biceps.

She'd tried to forget him, had lied to herself that it was just a one night stand. But the fantasies had persisted, and now, seeing him in the flesh, her body was flaring with desire.

"I am not at liberty to discuss Danergy's future plans at this moment," she said with a practiced smile, before turning to the rest of the reporters. "Thank you for your interest, gentlemen, but I do have an appointment to keep. Please follow up with my office if you have further questions."

Not waiting for any response, she hightailed it up the Capitol steps to the cool marble corridors, quickly finding the women's restroom to hide in a stall.

She whipped out her phone and stared at it. What the hell was she thinking?

Clearly she wasn't. Or at least her head wasn't. Some other part of her anatomy was definitely in charge.

A surge of excitement pulsed through her veins as her thumbs flew across her keypad. She quickly hit *send* before her brain could protest.

KACE CROSSED HIS ANKLE over his knee as he sat in Senator Mike Harris' waiting room. He was early for his appointment. He probably should review his prepared statement, maybe jot down some questions. Or maybe page through a magazine. Or check his phone for messages.

Anything to stop thinking about Madison in a cute pink suit.

Of course she was in D.C. He knew she would be. He just hadn't expected to see her all pink and perfect.

He uncrossed his legs and shifted in the upholstered office chair. It was just too damn bad she was on the wrong side of all of this. She was an intelligent woman. She must know she was on the wrong side.

Or maybe he could convince her?

He sighed in defeat and stared at the magazine rack.

Curiosity over what was going on in his small corner of the world won out over a very old copy of *Smithsonian.*

He pulled his phone out of his briefcase, the notification light flashing. Probably Paris checking in on him.

Yep, a text.

But not from Paris.

From Madison.

He looked around. No one was watching him. Of course not. He was just a constituent as far as anyone in the office knew, not some guy banging his political enemy.

I'd like to see you. Tell me where you're staying. I'll wear a disguise.

He could say no. He *should* say no.

Instead he told her the name and address of his hotel and that he'd be back there around five p.m.

His thumb did not hesitate to hit send. But his gut cramped the moment the message zipped into the ether.

CHAPTER SEVEN

Wearing oversized, dark sunglasses in a hotel lobby in D.C., even on a summer evening, should have raised more eyebrows. But the desk clerk only glanced and did not bat an eye as Madison walked across the worn oriental carpet to press the brass elevator button. Her scalp itched under her wig, and the tendrils of the synthetic hair tickled her cheeks as her head scarf pressed them against her face.

The elevator stopped with a *ca-chunk*. She pulled open the outer and inner scissor gates and stepped inside, the thumping of her heart drowned out by squeaking metal as she closed the gates. Luckily she was alone, so no need for small talk with strangers inside the gleaming wooden car.

The elevator lurched, then stopped. She steadied herself, then grabbed the inner gate, ready to wrench it open, before catching a glimpse of the historic plaque above the panel of buttons. Apparently the resident ghost, a Mr. Fouch, might cause the elevator to not function if he were suspicious of a caller or protective of a guest.

Madison rolled her eyes. A moment later, the elevator jerked and clunked on its way up. Okay, so she must have passed some paranormal test. She laughed inwardly. Why didn't Kace just stay in a modern hotel? He probably liked the experience of being mired in history. With a ghost, to boot.

On the fourth floor the elevator stopped. She struggled with the gates—going *mano-a-mano* with Mr. Fouch, who relented after a few choice expletives. A short walk down the shabby corridor and she was at Kace's door, her scalp overheated from nervousness and the stupid wig.

She knocked and removed her sunglasses. He opened the door, a blank look glazing his eyes momentarily until recognition dawned on him. One corner of his mouth twitched upward as his lips thinned, clearly an attempt to not laugh.

He beckoned her inside and closed the door.

"A wig?" he said with a muffled laugh. "And a babushka?"

"Babushka?"

"What my mother called—" he waved a hand at her head, "a scarf like that." He shook his head with a grin. "I guess you know best how to disguise yourself. I saw all those reporters around you today. I had no idea you were so famous."

She took off her scarf. "I've been in all the celebrity magazines."

He raised a brow. "Oh?"

"Haven't you heard of Brock Branson?"

"The guy in those action movies?"

"Yeah, him."

He scoffed. "Of course."

"I was married to him."

"Really?" Kace gaped. "So, I guess it didn't work out, huh?"

"Not so much." Madison placed her purse on top of an antique chest of drawers.

"Wasn't he just in the news for some reason?"

"I don't think so." Although she wouldn't be at all surprised.

"I think I read an article about him in a magazine at the dentist's office. Like his kid almost drowned at the beach?"

"Oh. Yeah. That was a while ago." And the story was fake. A way to print photos of him bare-chested, his arm around his bikini-clad hot young wife. And to remind the world he had a kid.

Something she had failed to provide him when they were married.

"I guess I went to the dentist a while ago."

Madison grabbed the cap of the wig and tugged.

"Whoa, whoa, whoa." Kace held up a hand. "What are you doing?"

"Taking this damn thing off."

"Black suits you. I think." He gave her the once over and played with draping the hair over her shoulders. "And besides there's something sexy about a lover wearing a disguise. It's like being with a different woman. Being with a stranger."

Lover? Were they lovers? They were, weren't they? That's why she went through all the trouble to meet up with him.

"I don't know how to respond to that. I suppose that's your kink?"

"I didn't realize how arousing it was until just now." Kace glanced at her mouth and licked his lips.

He wanted her. But he stood before her tense, frozen, not doing anything about it.

Because he was a gentleman despite the one-time display of brutish masculinity and his just-now brazen confession of wanting her to role play being a stranger.

She flipped the black tresses over her shoulders, then looped her arms around his neck. "So tell me, Mr. Park Ranger, do you invite strange women to your hotel room often?"

"I—" He stopped his protest and pursed his lips, perusing her face. Suddenly, his expression softened into cool confidence. "Not often enough."

He grabbed her at the waist and pressed his mouth to hers, his tongue plunging inside, dizzying her and loosening her grasp of reality. Being in his arms was so comfortable, so gratifying…

So dangerous.

She should stop him, should stop them. But, *oh*, it was so good, so right, their bodies arcing, fitting together like pieces of a puzzle, as if they were meant to be together, the hardness in his jeans the perfect counterpoint to the softness dampening her panties.

Kace pulled away, leaving her bereft, his chest rising and falling with heaving breaths.

"I should unpack," he said between huffs.

"You haven't unpacked?"

"I got in late this morning just in time for meetings."

"Oh."

"And I'm hungry."

"I'll order room service."

He laughed. "I don't think this place has room service."

Madison grabbed her burner phone, picked up precisely for her illicit liaison. "Then I'll call for delivery. What're you in the mood for?"

"Anything I can't find in the middle of nowhere."

"Such as?"

"Turkish, Indian, Ethiopian…"

"Sushi?"

That made him grin. "That sounds wonderful and expensive."

"I'm paying."

He sighed and heaved his bag onto the bed. "All right. Sushi."

She called her favorite D.C. Japanese take-out spot and ordered sushi and a bottle of their finest sake. Make that two bottles.

When dinner had been taken care of, she sat cross-legged on the bed and watched him unpack. A uniform. A couple of shirts. Underwear. Toiletries.

"Is that all you brought?"

"I'm not like you. I live simply." He winked. "And I don't need a disguise."

"What are you wearing for the hearing?"

"My service uniform."

She stared at him, incredulous.

"Not what I wear to work. My dress uniform. I wear it when I represent the NPS in an official capacity."

She shook her head. "No, no, no, no. You can't wear that."

"And why the hell not?" Indignation was smoothed over with disbelief.

"Because if you want to make your case before a committee that is already set against you, you cannot appear as the 'other'. You have to appear as one of them."

"A member of Congress?"

"Yes, in a tailored suit and tie."

He shook his head. "I've appeared before Congress before dressed in my army uniform with no problem. In fact, I would say I garnered a shit ton of respect."

"That's different. Everyone respects veterans. They have to. Even the fanatical right and fringe left."

He chuckled. "If that's so, everyone should respect those who serve our wonderful country in any way they choose." He glared at her. "Even as mere National Park Service employees."

"Yes, but you'd look so good in a tailored suit."

"I haven't worn a suit since my high school prom."

An image of eighteen-year-old Kace flashed in her brain. Her nipples tightened at the thought.

He noticed and raised a brow.

She drew her knees up to her chest.

"Madison," he said gently, "I have to wear my dress uniform at the hearing. It's required of my position."

"Okay." She sighed in resignation. "So put it on."

A crease formed between his graying eyebrows. "Now?"

"Yeah. I want to see."

"Fuck." He threw up his hands, then proceeded to undress down to his undershirt and briefs, a state he stayed in for far too short a time before he layered on his uniform.

Yikes. Atrocious. He looked…frumpy.

"Kace, you can't wear that. I won't let you."

"You won't *let* me?"

"I mean, look at the pants. They're bunching at your ankles. And that jacket. You're swimming in it."

"I'm big in certain places. I had to get the next size up from my usual size."

"I'll say."

There was that glare again.

Madison got up and grabbed her phone. He needed a tailor.

"A tailor?"

Oops. Did she just say that out loud?

"Madison, the suit is fine. And I can't afford a tailor."

"It's on me."

"I can't accept gifts from you. You know that. It's unethical. It's bad enough you're buying me dinner. And that we've slept together."

That stung. "So, is me buying you dinner, or fronting the bill for tailoring, or even sleeping with you going to change your mind about Danergy fracking at Fort America?"

"Oh, God no."

"I thought as much." She turned her attention to her real phone and opened her contacts. "And don't worry. It'll be so discreet the Russians won't know about it."

That got him to chuckle.

Found him. Good ole Saul Kleid who'd never told anyone about her weight changes when he had to let out her designer dresses. His discretion and skill were worth the airfare from D.C. to Hollywood.

She glanced at Kace who was busy changing clothes. "How many days do we have?"

"One," he said as he slid into his polo shirt. "I have meetings tomorrow at ten thirty and two p.m. The committee hearing is the day after, at eleven."

She pursed her lips. "Alright. We can do this. I'll have Saul come tomorrow morning at eight for the first fitting. He should be able to get it done in a day." Saul had always loved her like an uncle would. Or a real dad. He'd do it.

Kace grunted as he tugged on his jeans. "Sounds like a lot of work. Why bother?"

"Because, as much as I'm on the other side in all of this, I like you. And I love to see a man in a killer suit as much as I love to see him out of it."

He flicked his gaze at her wig. "Next you'll want me to dye my hair."

"Not on your life. The gray is distinguished and photogenic." Not to mention sexy as hell.

A knock on the door was her cue to get off the bed and motion to Kace to retreat to the bathroom.

"I'm paying, remember? And I'm disguised. Best not let the delivery guy know whose room this is. Lots of gossip in this town."

*****

KACE HADN'T HAD SUSHI since…well, he couldn't remember the last time. But he remembered enough to discern that this was the best sushi he'd ever had.

And the best damn sake.

He downed the remnants in his hotel glass. "How much was this?" He held up the bottle.

Across the small table before the hotel room window, Madison stuffed her mouth full of spicy tuna roll. She chewed a bit. "Does it matter?"

"I suppose not. Just curious."

She watched as he poured another glass. She swallowed as he took a sip. "One hundred and fifty dollars."

He spat out what was in his mouth.

"And that was about five dollars-worth right there," she said laughing.

"And you ordered two bottles?"

"They're small bottles. You're a big guy."

Kace stared at the milky liquid in his glass. "Jesus. I had no idea food could cost so much."

A smile played upon her lips. "Welcome to my world."

The excess of it all. He could never get used to that. "All bought by oil money, right?"

"Ultimately, I suppose," she said, stuffing her mouth with yellowtail nigiri. "In my case, I took what was given me and invested it very well."

"So you could have money to invest in more oil."

Madison pointed a chopstick in his direction. "That was never my intention." She chewed. "And I mean that. The opportunity just arose so I went for it."

"What was your intention?"

She gazed at her plate and let out a heavy sigh. "I always imagined myself a philanthropist, I suppose. But that was when I was married to Brock. You know, it looks good. Famous actor and his wife doing something for kids not as privileged as theirs."

"You have kids?" He hadn't even thought Madison could be a mother. But if she'd been married before—

"No." She took a gulp of sake. "That's why I'm divorced." Another gulp. "Because I couldn't."

The sadness in her voice was reflected in her eyes.

"Madison." He reached across the table. "I'm sorry. I didn't know."

She gave his hand a squeeze. "Of course you didn't." She pulled her hand away to wipe an eye. "You don't go to your dentist often enough."

He laughed at her grim joke.

"So here I am, unmarried and childless. I'll garner far more respect as a single woman when I head up the first joint public-private mining operation than some children's charity."

A much-welcomed cool breeze fluttered the curtains as Kace stared at her. She was dead serious, that was certain. Even wealth did not make a woman an equal to a man.

"So you see why this is so important to me, Kace."

Yes, he did see.

He nodded and took another swig of stupidly expensive sake. They truly inhabited different worlds with different goals and different amenities. He inhaled and gathered his thoughts.

"If you always imagined yourself a philanthropist, why don't you concentrate more on your foundation? Helping other women achieve success seems like it might be a better way to get respect. And then, you know, you could do TED talks and write a book."

That brought a smile back to her lovely face. "You just really don't want me fracking your land, do you?"

"Well, no, of course I don't." He chewed on a piece of pickled ginger. "But there's a larger philosophical issue here."

"Philosophical, Dr. Jaager?" A raised brow suggested she had put up her bullshit detector.

"I'm not going to lecture you. But you call yourself a feminist and I think you might be overlooking the important intersection of environmentalism and feminism."

She rolled her eyes. "You mean like how women are 'in tune with Mother Earth'?"

"No. Well, a spiritual component certainly pops up in some discourse, and is often used metaphorically. You know the whole male-dominated energy companies raping the earth is like men's oppression of women."

"Kace," she warned, "that argument goes nowhere with me."

"I know, I know." He organized his thoughts. "I'm talking about how women, including corporate executives like yourself, do not have an equal number of seats at the decision-making table, as it were. So when it comes to environmental policy-making or planning or involvement in industry, women will be left behind."

"I'm listening, professor."

"First, I need to listen to you. I'm assuming you have marketing statistics memorized."

"Some, yeah."

"Do you know the percentage of women CEOs in the oil and gas industry?"

"Hmm. It's like one percent." She thinned her lips.

"And solar?"

A raised eyebrow. "Now why did I know you were going to ask that?"

"Because you're smart."

She grinned. "It's still not much. Around five percent, I think."

"So clearly men dominate the oil and gas industries. More so than solar. What about other alternative energy industries? If your goal is to promote women, why not promote them where the glass ceiling is more like a partially open window?"

She glanced away briefly, as if in thought, then met his gaze. "But isn't that what men want? For women to admit defeat and move along? To stop banging on the window of the oil company's corner office, and grab the next best thing?"

"Okay, yeah, very definitely the patriarchy—"

Another eye roll.

"—wants women to shut up and sit down in a corner. But if you're completely out of earshot, then they have no control over you, right?"

She crossed her arms over her chest and exhaled.

"Alternative energy is still a nascent industry in the US compared to oil and gas." He poked a chopstick in a small dish of wasabi. "And, I know you don't want to believe this, but it's the wave of the future. One way for business women to be in charge is to take charge of industries ignored by men."

Madison sat back and tucked her lower lip between her teeth, her mind seemingly churning. "All right. You've given me something to think about. But I have to be honest, Kace. I'm not going to abandon this project. It's too important right now. Besides, my dad has given me a seat at the decision-making table, as you put it. In fact, he's put me at the head of it."

"Yeah, I get it." Kace sliced a chopstick in the air. "Lecture over. Class dismissed."

Madison chortled as she absently stirred her soy sauce. A breeze ruffled the hairs of her wig. "So, what made you pick this hotel?"

"It's a favorite of Park Service employees when we have to be in D.C. It fits our budget."

"Too bad you don't have a balcony like mine. We could finish that second bottle outside. It's a nice evening."

"Ah, but then we might be seen together. I'm only on the fourth floor and camera lenses are pretty high-powered these days."

"So..." She stood and came around the back of his chair. "I suppose that means we have to spend time inside your hotel room." She draped herself over him, wrapping her arms around his neck.

"Madison, what are you doing?" Both his body and brain knew damn well what she was doing, he just needed to hear her say it.

"We're attracted to each other," she said softly, her breath warm on his earlobe. "Let's take this opportunity while we have it."

With a turn of his head, he found her mouth waiting, her lips moist and parted. He kissed her, just a taste, a prelude to what he hoped would transpire later.

He stood and enveloped her briefly in his arms. "I have an idea." He padded across the room to turn off the light. On his return, he took her by one hand, grabbing the bottle of sake with the other.

"Come."

Kace led her to the side of the bed near the window. He sat on the floor and leaned against the bed, and motioned for her to do the same. She sat despite the tight jeans.

"Look." He pointed to the evening sky through the window, sunset streaking the blue with gold and orange. "Not a balcony but a view nonetheless."

She chortled and toed off her shoes, then curled up against him.

The image of them sitting serenely on a balcony somewhere in Europe, like the one he'd had in Paris on the Seine after his service, enjoying a nice bottle of wine, flitted through his head. A dream life far and away from this bizarre reality of impending doom while getting off with the enemy.

He tipped back the bottle. The cold bite of sake emboldened him.

"If your tailor will be here at eight tomorrow morning, why don't you just spend the night?"

*****

MADISON STIFFENED. Had Kace really just said what she thought he'd said?

"I mean, only if it fits your schedule. Busy business woman and all."

Yep. He had. The rapid pounding of her heart was making it difficult to breathe normally. The lingering heat of the day did not help either.

"I'd love to stay, Kace. Your appointment with Saul is the earliest item on my agenda."

He wrapped an arm around her, and offered her the sake. She took a swallow and handed it back.

"You finish it."

"Really?"

"Yes," she said with a laugh at his incredulity. "I can have hundred-dollar wine anytime."

He raised the bottle to the view out the window. "To Madison. I wish your good fortune was not at my expense."

"I wish it wasn't either." He was a nice guy. Besides being sexy as hell.

Kace drank the sake like a thirsty man in the desert, then plunked the bottle on the nightstand. "Why does it have to be?"

Shit. She shouldn't tell him. But she wanted to. He was too genuine a man to want to deceive. "It was either Fort America or somewhere else with shale reserves. The senators and representatives and mining industry executives chose your site because it's remote and relatively unknown."

"Yeah. We're like Yosemite and Grand Canyon combined, but no one's ever heard of us."

"Sadly, yes. But other factors were taken into account. It was determined your eponymous fort, for instance, would be able to withstand the tremors associated with wastewater injection."

"Jesus." Kace ran a hand down his face. "Whereas the rock formations at Arches National Park would crumble. Okay, I get it."

Madison drew back from his embrace. "Kace, I'm sorry. I'm sorry that it's you and that it's me…and now I'm sounding like a whiny kid and not a CEO." She slumped against the bed.

Kace sighed and pulled her to him. "On the bright side, we would've never met otherwise."

"I suppose." She pouted.

He kissed the top of her head. Which reminded her she still wore the hideous wig.

"Damn," he muttered.

"What?"

"I didn't think to pack condoms." He gave her a squeeze. "You don't suppose you could get some delivered?"

She shrugged him off to fetch her purse and dug in. She knelt before him and held up a handful of square wrappers.

His jaw dropped. "Jesus, you're that horny?"

"No," she laughed. "Just prepared and hopeful. They might be kind of old." She tossed the condoms on the nightstand and plopped down on the floor beside him. "You still want me after what I just told you?"

He sighed. "You're not an evil person, Madison. I don't agree with your views in the slightest. You'll never convince me that what you're proposing is necessary or good. But, despite all of that, I'm amazingly attracted to you. And, like you said, we should take the opportunity to explore that attraction."

She leaned in and pressed her lips to his, kissing him with an audible *smack*.

"And once you start fracking my land, I'll be too annoyed to want to fuck you. So get it while the getting's good."

She gripped his polo shirt to move in for another kiss but he was too quick for her. And too strong. He grabbed her by the waist and lifted her off the floor and onto the bed.

God, that was hot.

He straddled her, his arousal evident, the hunger on his face reflecting that need. She slowly rubbed the bulge at his crotch. He grew harder under her touch.

He reached for his waistband. She stilled his hand.

"Nope. Only when I say. Or when I do."

A throaty growl rumbled through him.

She raised herself on her elbows, her face at the level of his crotch. She pressed her mouth to the ridge of his erection and exhaled.

Kace sucked air through his teeth, his hands flexing at his sides.

Madison scooted up to sitting. She met his gaze as she yanked open the top button of his waistband.

He licked his lips and narrowed his eyes.

She tugged on his fly. One by one, each button popped free. She reached through the Y of his briefs and pulled out his erection.

Still holding his gaze, she opened her mouth.

A juddering gasp was followed by a string of hopeful encouragements.

She wrapped her lips around his hardness. Encouragements changed to sputtered expletives. She slid her tongue along the underside of his shaft. The expletives turned to prayers.

Madison grabbed his butt as she took him further into her mouth, the tip grazing the back of her throat, squeezing his length as she drew back, each motion deliberately slow, wanting to torture him with her lazy rhythm.

One hand still holding on to him, she unbuttoned her jeans and slid her fingers inside to rub her clit, flinching from unexpected sensitivity. *Jeez,* she was wet. And extremely slippery. And super horny.

She released his cock with a taunting *pop,* keeping her gaze locked on his. She lay back against the pillows and continued masturbating, her panties completely soaked now. His chest heaved as he watched her, his cock standing at attention.

She drew her tongue across her upper lip then nodded.

Apparently, that was all he needed. He grabbed the ankles of her jeans and pulled. They *were* tight. Madison laughed as she helped strip them off.

His jeans were a little easier to remove. His briefs, polo, and t-shirt were quickly dispensed with, as well. After posing and showing off his pecs, he challenged her with a glower. She shed her top and bra immediately.

"Black lace. Nice."

She fell back on the bed, flopping an arm over her head.

Crap. She was still wearing that damn wig.

She grabbed the crown.

Kace stopped her. "Oh, no. You're not taking that off. I like it."

"Really?"

"Yeah. Like I said before, it's like being with a stranger." He gave her the once over. "Maybe from France."

France? A memory? Well, if so, she'd have to give his past lover a run for her money.

Madison posed on the bed like a porn star.

That did the trick.

Kace urged apart her knees, a hungry look in his eyes as he stared at her crotch.

He grabbed a condom from the nightstand and ripped it open, his thick fingers fumbling for a split second with the delicate wrapper. He raised an eyebrow at her as he unrolled it over his bobbing erection.

Arousal flared between her legs. She was more ready than she'd ever been.

He aimed his cock and pushed in, his groan an undertone to her sigh of contentment.

His gaze locked with hers, his expression softened as his movements slowed.

Tender, almost tentative, caresses curved along her breasts, her abdomen, her hips, sliding under her butt. A tilt of her pelvis emboldened him to wrap an arm around her, pulling her close. Their union was a slow dance at first, rhythmic, gradually building until they moved as one, like dancers skilled in the tango, able to perform with a partner of equal experience.

His free hand snaked down her body until he found her clit. Gentle strokes took her on a languorous journey, her mind spinning and whirling under his sensual control, her body undulating in their lover's dance.

His grunts filled her ear, his hot exhalations lay humid against her neck, growing faster, faster, as he picked up his pace. He pressed his thumb against her clit, unleashing a mind-blowing orgasm, her cry of ecstasy his cue to slam inside, taking his pleasure now that she'd had hers.

Such a gentleman.

One last thrust. He stilled the moment he came, his body flexing and jittering in his silent release, a faraway look haunting his expression.

Had he been thinking of his dark-haired lover from long ago? Trying to ignore the fact his actual lover was about to crush his corner of the world?

Madison's heart sunk.

He slumped on top of her, his heaving chest pressing into her, the fine hair tickling her nipples.

Tomorrow she would order breakfast and make sure that uniform fit him like he was born to wear it. Then they would go their separate ways, to meetings about opposite sides of the same issue, each wondering about what the hell they had done the night before.

Or maybe only she would wonder such a thing.

Madison closed her eyes, staunching the tears that threatened to ruin a wonderful sensual moment in the arms of a man she was feeling far too much for.

CHAPTER EIGHT

Two days later

Kace stared out the window of Zara's Café in D.C.'s Woodridge neighborhood, a place far from the politics of Capitol Hill where no one would go looking for him. He especially needed to avoid the media after the shitshow that had been the hearing before the Senate Committee on Energy and Natural Resources.

He sipped his cappuccino then stared at the foam, bubbles scattering in the wake of his consuming assault.

The hearing had been the most exhausting three hours of his life. An emotional roller coaster that had left him physically drained. Three hours of interrogation by a panel of antagonistic senators could do that to a man.

A wave of respect rippled through him for those who'd had to endure far more than a mere three hours before such hectoring lunkheads.

Maybe it wouldn't have been so horrible if the three hours hadn't've been an utter and total waste of time. As if they fully intended to pass S.3806 and had just been going through the motions of the democratic process.

But, clearly everything had been stacked against him. Everyone had seemed annoyed by his very presence.

After the hearing, disgusted and furious, he'd high-tailed it back to his hotel to tear off his exquisitely tailored uniform and slap on some jeans and a t-shirt. For effect he grabbed his green NPS zip-up bomber jacket, minus his name tag, then took off to a part of town no white senator would be caught dead in.

The waitress hovered her coffee pot over his cup.

"Oops. You got one of those fancy drinks."

He smiled at her. "Go ahead. I need it. Even in this heat."

She smiled back. "This town does that to people, doesn't it?"

He snorted a response. Then turned his attention to the scenes of normal life out the window. People who were oblivious to the plights of embattled park rangers.

First the committee chair had mispronounced his name. People always mispronounced his name. He should have anticipated it and let it slide right off him.

But it got to him. Senators had staff to apprise them of what to expect at hearings. Clearly they hadn't listened. The chair exaggerated the erroneous "ee" in an almost mocking way.

"Keece…what sort of name is that?"

"*Kace*—" he politely emphasized the correct pronunciation "—is Dutch. Sir."

A scoff followed. As if a Dutch heritage was somehow distasteful. As if being the son of an immigrant in a nation of immigrants was objectionable.

They asked if he was married, and when he said he was not, they asked if he ever had been. In the moment, why such a thing mattered was beyond Kace. He'd responded he had never been married. An ensuing remark about a rugged man in his prime having never been married was laden with insinuation. It only dawned on him later that his sexuality had been in question, and, therefore, to these committee members and their voter base, his credibility.

"Dr. Jaager, you have an advanced degree in archaeology, correct?"

"Yes, sir."

"Yet you've never actually found any evidence of slave occupation, or even Native American occupation, during the archaeological field schools at the Fort America site, have you?"

As the "purported" history of Fort America was addressed, Kace's gut had churned.

The whiteness—and the maleness—of the panel of senators before him came into full focus. He felt compelled to combat that fact with his response.

"Fort America hosts an archaeological field school every summer which searches for evidence of occupation of African-Americans seeking freedom and the Native Americans who helped them. The field school will continue the search until evidence of the existence of people who did not want to be found is found."

Then they asked him about his time in the army.

"You were in Desert Storm, were you not?"

"Yes, sir."

"And, I think I speak for the committee in thanking you for your service to our country."

"You're welcome, sir."

"Now, Dr. Jagger—"

For the second time Kace had to correct the pronunciation of his last name. *Not like the rock star? No sir, the 'a' is long.*

"We all know that part of the world, the Middle East, is unstable," said the chair. "Especially now with terrorists everywhere. Don't you think it should be national policy to make sure we are not beholden to countries that support terrorism? Isn't that what you fought for?"

He explained he had fought to send a message to a dictator, that he could not run roughshod over a sovereign nation, a nation that was an ally to the United States.

This history appeared to have been lost on the distinguished gentleman. The senator had looked a bit perplexed. "You mean Saddam Hussein and Iraq?"

"No, sir, I mean Saddam Hussein's invasion of Kuwait."

But Kace had also fought to save the birth place of Western civilization from further violence. The effort had proved to be futile.

"Of all people, a veteran of the Gulf War must understand the United States needs to create a strategy to maintain energy independence, of energy dominance, even, and to achieve that strategy, we must explore all sources of energy for our country."

At that point, Kace politely mentioned that sources of energy could be found by exploiting the sun, wind, geothermal, and waves.

But he was shot down. Because a supervisor of a National Park was not an expert in energy matters.

Then why the hell had he been asked to testify before the goddamn Energy Committee?

Kace's phone buzzed. A text. From Bettina.

Saw you on C-SPAN. We'll fight this, Kace. p.s. Looking good in that uniform!

He chuckled.

I'm taking refuge in your favorite coffee shop, he texted back. *Don't tell C-SPAN.*

Bettina responded with a photo. *You know you got your own hashtag?*

Shit, really? He enlarged the photo, a screenshot from Twitter of the latest tweets tagged #SaveFortAmerica next to a picture of him testifying. Every single Rogue account had posted it. Paris was on the ball.

That elicited such a wide grin he looked around to make sure no one thought he might be crazy. No one took any notice.

Made my day. Thanks Bett.

He got a thumbs-up and a smiley face in return.

Kace sat back and actually enjoyed his next swallow of coffee-cino. Inside the café and out on the street patrons and passersby minded their own business. No one cared about his plight, about the plight of a chunk of rock with beautiful views and a landscape with awe-inspiring sunsets.

Each one of these people had plenty else on their minds. And that was part of the problem, wasn't it?

While people struggled to get jobs, to pay their bills on minimum wage, to get accepted because of their race or gender or gender identity, to find someone to take care of their kids at an affordable price, to find a fricking place to live in a tight housing market...

His problem was nothing, NOTHING, compared to what normal people had to deal with every goddamn day.

All he had to contend with was some hot chick wanting to frack near his office. No one cared about Fort America. Hardly anyone knew it even existed. They were all at Yosemite or, *Jesus*, San Juan fucking Island.

His phone buzzed again. A text.

From Madison.

Fuck.

He closed his eyes, imagining her teasing him, moments later in his arms, writhing and moaning, sharing mutual pleasure. He'd tried to imagine it was someone else underneath him, but she was too perfect, and they were too good together.

Regret mixed with irritation pulsed through him as he pressed the message icon.

She said she thought he had exhibited honorableness and had performed quite well under pressure.

The pressure that only existed because of her.

Can I see you tonight?

He stared at her message, unsure what to say.

Unsure what he felt.

Madison had not spent the previous night with him. After the final fitting of his uniform, she'd left. Dinner with her father and his cronies, she had said.

And then seeing her outside the hearing room that morning had just about bowled him over. She had been surrounded by politicians and press and industry leaders—all men—each listening to whatever it was she had to say. Amidst the fuss, she had appeared poised, confident, and, as always, impeccably dressed.

They all wanted her. But, to them, she was untouchable. Only Kace got to have her. And *she* wanted *him*.

Bring dinner, he texted back. *6:00*.

MADISON PLOPPED the cardboard takeaway container on the tiny cafe-style table tucked by the window of Kace's hotel room and began to unpack the smaller boxes.

Kace leaned over and took a whiff. "Smells good," he enthused. "What's for dinner?"

"Lots of wonderful stuff from my favorite French takeout place."

"French takeout? I had no idea there was such a thing."

"There is, and you'll love it."

As she opened the boxes of herbed new potatoes, steak with mushroom sauce, roasted zucchini and eggplant, she watched him from the corner of her eye. He paced the narrow strip of carpet between the bed and the table, like a caged animal craving freedom. She calmly set out the paper plates and tableware.

"It's compostable. I figured you'd like that."

He gave her a faraway look. "What is?"

She waved at the spread. "Well, everything I suppose. Including the knives and forks."

She fetched glasses from the bathroom and poured the wine. She handed him a glass. "Looks like you could use this."

"Thanks." He took a swallow. "How much was this?" He nodded at the wine bottle.

"Kace," she scolded.

"I just want to know."

"Fifty dollars. Cheap." She sighed. "Sit. You're making me nervous with all that walking back and forth."

"Sorry. It's been a nerve-racking day." He took his place at the table and stared at the food. "Jesus, this looks good."

"Dig in."

They hadn't said a word to each other about the hearing, about how he had not been treated with the respect Madison had requested of the committee members. Little things, like how she had told the committee chair how to pronounce Kace's name. They'd mispronounced it deliberately, to make him feel self-conscious and unsure of himself. She'd complained to the senators and to Dad afterward, but they'd shrugged it off as "politics as usual".

She should probably tell Kace—

"I don't want to talk about it, Madison. Just so we're clear." He continued to look at his dinner rather than in her direction.

"All right." She concentrated on her steak, the tender meat perfectly seasoned.

He cut and chewed with vigor. "This is the best steak I've ever had."

Okay. Food. They could talk about food.

"Sometimes I imagine you attending lots of picnics with master barbecuers. You know, like after a hike or something."

He let out a bland chuckle. "In my early days with the Park Service, I was stationed at Canyonlands with a bunch of kids my age. We had our fair share of competitive cookouts."

"Do you like working at remote places?"

"I do. I'm not much of a people person."

Although he had been perfectly diplomatic at the hearing given the way he'd been treated.

"I'm not sure I could handle being cut off from everything," she said instead.

"I see it as being more connected to everything." He finally looked her in the eye, his gaze intense. "Connected to the land, the air, wildlife, plants."

She swallowed her zucchini. "I guess I'm just a city girl at heart."

"Yet another thing that divides us."

He didn't specify whether he meant between them personally or professionally. Or both.

"Yes, but opposites attract sometimes, don't they?"

His lips twitched into a half-smile. "I suppose." He downed the rest of his wine and poured another glass. "Not bad for only fifty bucks."

She laughed, almost spewing a chunk of steak.

He raised a brow, the action making him even more devastatingly sexy. "You're still wearing the wig, you know."

"Makes it seem like you're having dinner with another woman." *Perhaps a French woman?*

"Admit it," he said with a gravelly quaver, "it was fun being a brunette in bed the other night."

"It's fun being with a man who likes to play around in the bedroom."

The eyebrows went up again, this time accompanied by a suggestive smirk that sent a tingle to tease her crotch. "And it's so great finding a woman who is willing to play around in the bedroom."

"I guess given how remote you are, you can't just sign up for online dating."

"I can, but then it's just sexting. Few are brave enough to venture to the middle of nowhere to get laid."

"Then you're lucky to have met me."

"And you're lucky I made a pass at you."

She giggled through a mouthful of vegetables. He was right. As much as she had been so pissed with him at the time, that kiss had knocked her socks off.

"What do you think about public sex?"

Madison froze, a forkful of potatoes poised before her mouth. "As in watching or partaking?"

Kace let out a guffaw. "Brilliant answer." He wiped the corners of his eyes. "Partaking."

A frisson of terror tinged with excitement crawled up the back of her neck. "I'm generally very cautious in public. You know, the paparazzi. They'd love to get a photo of me *in flagrante delicto*."

"They won't recognize you. You'll be wearing your wig and I can loan you a jacket, even a ball cap." He leaned back. "And you'll be with me. No one knows who I am. Despite being the star of C-SPAN today."

It was ridiculous to even consider. So why was her heart racing at the idea?

He took her hand. "It would be nice to take an evening stroll, don't you think?"

"It would," she conceded. "But let's wait until it gets a little darker."

AS THEY WALKED ALONG the Washington Mall near the Lincoln Memorial, Kace inhaled the stale, humid city air, a hint of Madison's exotic perfume adding a sensual note.

Without her high heels, Madison fit snuggly under his arm. And she could keep pace very well. In fact, she was following his lead perfectly.

Like she was under his control.

The notion struck a chord deep inside, rippling desire to his crotch.

Their relationship was nothing like that, though. In bed they were equals. She had as much control as he. Perhaps more, since he needed to make sure she consented after his stupid boorishness.

And giving control to her was only fair since he could barely control the beast she unleashed within.

Too bad he couldn't have been a bit more of a raging beast at the hearing today, told the senators what he really thought about them, about their plan to desecrate pristine American open space. But no, he had to be the polite, deferential spokesman of the National Park Service.

Thereby letting the Service get trampled upon.

Had he truly represented the men and women who devoted their lives to protecting the stunning beauty of this great land? Men and women who were so passionately dedicated to protecting that which made the United States unique?

Or had he let them all down?

History would eventually judge him, but at that moment, his gut told him he had failed miserably.

And the woman in his embrace was the reason.

He should hate her, but he couldn't. Her beliefs were misguided, but her struggle to make it in a man's world was surely to blame for that. She had to do anything, and the anything she did was what she knew best. Mining for oil.

Madison sighed with an air of satisfaction. "It's a lovely evening, Kace." She untwined his arm from her shoulder to hold his hand instead. "Thanks for dragging me out into the world."

He raised her hand to his lips and kissed it. "You're welcome."

Together they had devised her disguise. The wig of course, plus she'd popped out the lenses in her designer sunglasses and wore the empty frames.

"Trust me, it's a thing," she'd said after he'd railed against the ridiculousness of the fashion and how everyone would know there were no lenses.

Over her clingy t-shirt-like dress, she wore his jacket, or rather, she swam in his jacket, rolled-up sleeves bulky around her slender wrists. All to give the appearance of the gallant boyfriend offering his date a defense against the cool night air.

And, from the disregard of tourists passing them along the path of the Reflecting Pool, they must have resembled a nondescript middle-aged couple out for an evening stroll.

But beneath that respectable exterior an irrepressible desire to do something completely dirty throbbed and roiled within Kace.

Perhaps this libidinous desire was driven by the fervent patriotism roused as they passed monuments to American history, mixed with frustration toward the woman at his side.

Ahead lay the lighted fountain of the World War II Memorial. "Did you realize the Mall was a National Park?"

She stiffened. "The whole Mall?" She turned her head to look back at the Lincoln Memorial.

"Yep. Run by the National Park Service."

"No, I did not know that," she admitted quietly.

"A park in the middle of a metropolitan area, reminding those who work in the city of the values and sacrifices of our forebears."

"That's a little heavy-handed, Kace."

"Maybe," he said as they walked through the plaza along the southern colonnade. "This part of the monument is dedicated to those who served in the Pacific theater. That's where my father served."

Madison stopped and looked up at him. "Your father was in World War Two? He must be in his nineties."

"He would be." Kace resumed strolling. "He died when he was in his eighties."

Madison snorted as she gazed at the lighted arcs of water in the central fountain. "And my father was able to pull strings to get out of Vietnam."

"Really? Can't say I blame him."

"Yeah. But was it the honorable thing to do? Of all the war memorials, the Vietnam one is the most difficult for me to look at. All those names. It's too real."

Kace gave her shoulders a squeeze. The morose conversation was a jarring juxtaposition to his throbbing sex drive. "I bet I can show you a monument you haven't seen."

He unwrapped his arm and grabbed her hand. Behind them, the Washington Monument loomed, the erect freedom of the obelisk mocking the boner straining against his jeans.

He picked up the pace along the ramp toward the Atlantic arch. No one was around. No one. Not even the personnel who guarded the Mall at night.

A devious smile tightened his face as he led her through the arch, then jerked to the left to press her up against the cold granite.

Madison gulped air, her body rigid, her gaze flicking side to side in fear. Or excitement?

Kace crushed a hip against her, holding her in place as he palmed a perfect breast under the jacket—*his* jacket, enveloping her with his scent, claiming her. Madison nibbled on her lower lip.

He pressed his mouth to hers, interleaving their lips, her astonished gape giving room for his questing tongue. He delved in, losing himself in the bolts of lust firing to his toes, ricocheting to his crotch. He rocked his erection against her now-yielding hip, craving relief, knowing he would not get it at that moment.

He stepped back and jerked her toward him. Perhaps a bit too forcefully.

"Kace?"

He answered her plea by grabbing her arm to lead her along the wide concrete path, the dull glow from lampposts lighting their way. A left turn had them tripping down stone steps to the lake, the gentle lapping of water a counterpoint to their brisk footfalls.

"Where are we?" Madison's voice held a tiny quiver.

"Constitution Gardens."

Two joggers whooshed passed, seemingly the only other people in the park. The noise of evening traffic along Constitution Avenue reminded him they were not truly alone.

A lamppost signaled the entrance to Signers Island.

"We turn here." His rasp barely masked his excitement.

Kace directed Madison to the left, their footsteps drumming along the wooden footbridge. Then another left, toward the view of the Washington Monument looming beyond, where a weeping willow offered shadowed privacy in the public park.

And a promise for what he had wanted to do for the past few hours.

He urged her against the tree trunk, hovering his mouth above hers. "You said you'd do it in public, right?"

"I did." Her breath fell in shallow puffs as she licked her lips.

"Well, that's what we're going to do. And we're going to do it my way."

He pulled off the fake glasses and dropped them into her purse, then went for her wig.

She grabbed his hands. "Kace, stop." The calmness in her voice belied the trepidation flickering in her eyes.

"I won't force you, Madison. But I want to do this my way."

"And what way is that?"

"Knowing precisely who it is I'm fucking."

MADISON swallowed hard.

His way. Without her wig. Leaving her true identity exposed in public.

Her true identity as the woman who had wronged him exposed.

Her mind quibbled with the implications as her body screamed it didn't care.

She wanted to fuck him.

She stripped off the wig, tore off the ponytail holder and the bobby pins, dropping the lot into her purse.

"All right. Your way."

Kace ripped open the button fly of his jeans and reached into his briefs, grabbing his cock, brandishing it to the night air.

Obviously, there would be no preliminaries.

Except whatever involved the condom he yanked from the inside pocket of the jacket she wore.

He grabbed a fistful of her hair holding her in place as he leaned a hip against her. He lifted the hem of her dress to finger and fumble with her underwear. "I should have made you take these off at the hotel."

The thin cotton, damp with her arousal, was not much of a deterrent. He pulled the wet crotch aside as he nudged the head of his cock along her slit. She held onto his shoulders as he lifted her thigh, then shoved inside her in one smooth stroke.

She gripped him instantly, sighing unwittingly, her body welcoming the offered sexual release against her mind's rebuke.

He ground her butt into the rough tree as he rammed in a syncopated rhythm, his masculine grunts blasting in her ear, resonating in her core. Her scalp burned where he gripped her hair. She relaxed into his fist offering some relief.

His need to control her was all too understandable. Kace's whole world had been turned upside down because of her. The hearing had clearly been too traumatic to talk about. But she knew what had happened. She'd been there watching. His values, his service, his heritage had all been disparaged unnecessarily.

And she was the root cause of the evil in his life. No wonder he needed to get his frustrations out with her unmasked.

He released her hair to cup a cheek, seeking her mouth, his kiss tentative, an admission his need was also fueled by desire, a desire echoing within her. A mini-orgasm flared, then fizzled.

With a grunt and a jerk Kace came. He rested his head against hers, his panting breaths hot and wet on her nose. She scrunched her eyes shut to bank back the tears.

No use. He noticed. He pulled out and released her. "God, Madison, I was too rough, wasn't I?"

"No, no. Don't think that. Please." She meant it. "Just too many emotions tonight."

"Yeah." He dispensed with the condom in a tissue.

It was over. She tugged off his jacket, then put on the glasses and wig. "I should go."

"Yeah." He sounded noncommittal. Or, perhaps, reluctant.

Tears stung her eyes. Luckily it was too dark for him to really notice.

"I'll walk you to Constitution Avenue. You can catch a cab back to your hotel."

They walked in silence for a spell. For too long, really. They'd been intimate, and not just physically.

Kace's hand bumped hers. She stretched her fingers, and for one brief shining moment, they walked hand-in-hand.

Like lovers do.

"I'm leaving in the morning." He sounded gruff.

"All right." What was she supposed to say?

Kace stopped, taking her hand in both of his. "Look, Madison, I shouldn't have to say this, and it sounds really cliché anyway, but what happened here in D.C. stays in D.C."

She didn't want to agree but it was the only course of action. "Okay."

"We're going to be seeing each other over the next few months…" He let out an exasperated sigh and released his hold on her. "Or years."

Months, please. She couldn't handle years.

"We can't ever talk about this." He gestured back and forth. "You know, what happened between us."

"Yeah, I know." But she would relive it as long as her memory would let her.

They walked the rest of the way in silence.

"I think we're here."

Constitution Avenue. Their separation point. As lovers.

As friends.

She wanted to reach out, touch him, hug him. Instead, Madison's arms hung rigidly, her hands flexing with yearning as she resisted the temptation before her.

Kace waved down a taxi, turning his back when the driver pulled over.

Concealing himself. Just as she was concealed by her disguise.

She got in the cab without saying a word. As they drove away, she turned around to see Kace still standing on the sidewalk, watching her go.

KACE TRIED TO MOVE, tried to walk away, but he was mesmerized by the sight of his lover—probably his best lover— driving away.

Only when she was no longer in his sight did reality descend.

Damn it. What had he done?

She'd consented, right?

Yeah, she had.

But, Jesus, did he have to be an utter brute about it?

Anger and frustration had reared their ugly heads while he'd held her down, controlling her, the desire to do so too strong, compensating for his lack of control over the situation.

And now she was gone. Next time he saw her she would be Ms. Danes and he would be Mr. Jaager.

Which was too damned bad. They were so good together.

Kace shook his head and chuckled grimly. How on earth a woman could be so smart and ambitious yet so wrong was beyond him.

The walk back to the hotel would help him to sort through thoughts and emotions, calm him down from the high of orgasm, anger, and regret.

CHAPTER NINE

Fort America, two weeks later

At the flat basin in the shade of Fort America's stratified canyon walls, Madison pulled her Escalade off to the side of the dirt road and parked.

The area should have been empty. Instead it was teeming with children.

Okay, maybe not *teeming* exactly, but there were a couple dozen at least running around. Plus a few adults keeping watch.

What the hell were they doing there? She was supposed to meet up with a crew of architects and engineers further on down the road. She couldn't have kids running around.

Must be some sort of ploy by Kace.

Shit. Madison had sworn she wouldn't think about him anymore. The sex was great and all, but she had a job to do and, well, Kace was a thorn in the side of that job.

And it was very clear from their last night together that Kace never wanted to see her again unless he had to.

She got out of the car and approached the group. She honed in on one of the adults, a young woman, a pretty blonde probably in her early twenties, who was not preoccupied with chasing a youngster.

"Hello." Madison extended her hand. "I'm Madison Danes with Danergy."

The pretty woman smiled and shook her hand. "Hi. I'm Ingrid, Ingrid Brookes. Did TFA send you?"

"TFA?"

"I guess not, then." Ingrid laughed. "We're with Teach for America. Sometimes the executive directors send out mentors and experts to lecture the kids."

"Oh." Madison shifted on her feet, digging her brand new hiking boots into the red dirt.

An African-American boy, maybe around ten years old, ran up to Ingrid and pulled on her jacket. "Miss Brookes, Mr. Stein's gonna teach us how to do bulldring. Please, pretty please, can I go?"

"Bouldering, Jimmie," Ingrid corrected. "Okay. But be careful or I'll never hear the end of it from your mom."

Jimmie was gone in a flash to follow a boisterous bunch heading over to a mound of boulders nestled in a clump of evergreens.

Most of the kids were non-white. A tow-headed boy stuck out like a sore thumb.

"Where're you all from?" asked Madison.

"I'm with the Los Angeles group." Ingrid smiled. "Some are with the Las Vegas group."

"Is this some special program?"

"Yeah. Kace has been instrumental in pulling this all together."

Kace. Suddenly Ingrid's blondness and prettiness came into sharp focus.

What the fuck? Madison checked herself. She had to stop thinking like that, had to tame the jealous streak. Brock's philandering had poisoned her against younger women. She was still trying to work through the muck left behind in the wake of her bitter divorce.

Besides, Kace wasn't hers. She didn't own him. Far from it. They were nothing to each other.

Except he had taken a piece of her heart on their last night together. His morose distractedness afterward indicated he had felt something as well.

"Oh? So this is a regular field trip?"

"Uh-huh," Ingrid responded casually, oblivious to the hurricane of emotion tearing through Madison. "We've been partnering with the National Park Service and Leave No Trace for a few years now. It's one of the reasons why I really wanted to do TFA."

"Leave No Trace?"

Ingrid's smile thinned, as if she were taken aback by Madison's ignorance. "They're a non-profit that promotes engaging responsibly with wilderness. They manage all the camping aspects of the field trip."

Camping? Last thing Madison needed was a bunch of kids running around for several days while she was trying to conduct meetings. "Where will you all be camping?" she asked politely.

"You know, the campsite near where the rangers live."

So nowhere near her proposed development site. Madison let out a sigh of relief as she watched the kids playing with raucous enthusiasm.

"It seems as if these children have never seen a tree before. Don't they have parks where they live?"

"They do. But urban parks have lots of concrete and ready-made infrastructure. To see this much open space where kids have to make nature their playground is life-changing."

"They seem well-behaved."

"Yes, we only bring the best students on trips such as this. Students who have at least a C-plus average."

Madison gaped. "C-plus?" She'd never have gotten away with even a B-minus when she was in school.

"A C-plus is pretty good for a kid who might not have eaten breakfast or might experience some sort of violence either in the home or in the neighborhood." Ingrid observed the children with genuine affection. "And when they get back home they do better, they really do. They're transformed by the experience."

"Do you take field trips to other places, or is Fort America the only one?"

"Oh, no. We go to other places, too."

Thank God. The teachers would just have to change their plans next year. Should not be a problem.

A rumbling from behind startled Madison to turn around. Half a dozen kids ran toward them.

"Miss Brookes! Miss Brookes!"

They stopped before Ingrid, laughing and panting, talking at once.

"Miss Brookes, there was a bird—"

"With like a mouse or something—"

"In its mouth!" This elicited a few *eeww*s.

"And then another bird crashed into it—"

"And they were all fighting and stuff in the air—"

"Tearing at the mouse—" This was accompanied by a reenactment.

"It was nasty!"

"And then one of them dropped it—"

"But they were still fighting!"

"Sweet!"

"Then Shawndell was going to get the mouse—"

"But we all screamed at him—"

"Because one of the birds was coming at him!"

"It swooped down and grabbed the mouse and flew away."

"It was sick!" A chorus of agreement indicated *sick* was something good. The boy who was apparently Shawndell did a victory dance.

Just then one of the girls noticed Madison. She scanned her up and down with big brown eyes. "Are you a ranger?"

Madison put on her professional smile. "No. I'm the president of an energy company."

"What's that?" piped up a boy.

"I run a company that provides power, like electricity and gas, so you can have lights in your house and drive a car."

The girl with big brown eyes tilted her head to the side. "Ranger Kace says energy comes from the sun."

Ranger Kace. How cute.

"Well…" Madison glanced at Ingrid. She'd have to choose her words carefully. "The sun can be a source of energy. There are a lot of other sources. Like oil."

"But how do you get the oil?"

"We pump it out of the ground."

"Could you use the sun for that?"

Out of the mouths of babes. "I'm not sure you could…"

But she wasn't so sure she couldn't.

"What are you doing *here*?"

Finding an age-appropriate explanation was a challenge. "Fort America has a lot of energy reserves underground. My company wants to explore that potential."

"Are you going to build a gas station here?"

"No, not quite," she said with a smile. "More like a factory."

"A factory?" Shawndell asked. "What about all the rocks and trees?" Worry infused his words.

"They'll still be here, too."

"My auntie works in a factory," said the girl with big brown eyes. "They make chocolate."

"Chocolate?" A bunch of kids squealed at once.

Another girl focused intently on Madison. "Ooh, ooh, are you going to make chocolate?"

This was amusing and all, but she really needed to continue on down the pitted, gravel road to meet with her architects and engineers. "Nothing as fun as that," she confessed. "We're going to make energy so *you* can build a chocolate factory."

That opened a lot of mouths, widened a lot of eyes. Madison nodded to the kids, said a good-bye to Ingrid and headed back to her SUV.

Okay. So Kace and his kids had got to her. Best she could do was compromise.

The kids wouldn't be getting their chocolate factory.

But she could do something to appease Kace.

"Jesus, Kace. You've been in a funk ever since you got back from D.C."

Kace looked up from holding his head in his hands on his desk. Paris was scowling at him. Rightfully so.

"Is it five o'clock yet?" he asked.

Paris shook her head. "Every woman in America—and, like, a gazillion dudes—would love to cheer you up right now."

Kace grunted. After the hearing, he'd become something of an Internet meme. A picture of him looking humble yet serious with hashtags #SilverFox, #swoon, #TheHeroWeNeed, and a few that made him blush, popped up all over social media. Paris assured him the women of America had discovered his "rugged good looks" all on their own and his sudden, fleeting celebrity status had nothing to do with the Rogue social media accounts.

"I don't want every woman in America—"

He stopped. He was going to say *I only want one woman*. Not something he should admit, though, like, ever.

Paris rolled her eyes and sighed heavily. "You slept with her again, didn't you?"

"You realize that's none of your business?"

"It sure is when my goddamn boss is acting like a zombie during work."

She was right. Kace groaned. "We lost. No, wait, that's not quite right. *I* fucking lost. I condemned Fort America and everything around it to fracking hell."

All while sleeping with the enemy.

Paris plopped down in the chair on the other side of his desk. "Okay, I'm going to say this only one more time, Kace. It wasn't you. The hearing was a sham. The damn Senate was always gonna pass S.3806."

"And now the bill's in the House. Still doesn't look good for us."

"Yeah, okay, you're right. But none of this was *your* fault, Kace. I just wish you would believe that."

His head ached way too much to be able to contemplate reason.

"How's about we make popcorn and watch a crappy flick from the nineties?"

He chuckled. "All right." Paris was a movie nerd. Had even been to film school. She'd figure out a way to take his mind off everything for a couple of hours.

"Good." Paris reached out and spread her hand on his desk. "I need you focused and present, boss." Emphasis on *boss*, clearly because he really hadn't been acting like one lately.

"Yeah. I know. I get it."

Five o'clock finally came. Paris climbed into Kace's Jeep and they drove to his house, she tossing out movie titles along the way, half of which he was certain he did not want to see.

"Okay, so no post-apocalyptic, dystopian crap. And no rom-coms. And no horror—"

Because all of those mirrored his own life way too much.

"James Bond? Like is there a Bond movie you haven't seen?"

The question hung in the air as they pulled up to his house, an all-too-familiar bright red Cadillac Escalade parked in front.

"Jesus H. Christ, Kace, what the fuck is *she* doing here?" Paris hissed, not concealing her annoyance.

What the fuck was right. Madison Danes was looking at his house, taking notes, taking photos, and, as always, wearing some tight-fitting outfit. This time, tight jeans and a low-cut top.

Shit.

If this was subterfuge for a booty call while she was destroying the future of Fort America, she was out of luck.

Kace pulled up, Paris jumping out of the car before he parked. She stood as a sentinel while he got out and approached his now-nemesis.

"Ms. Danes, may I help you?"

Madison met his eyes, surprise—and perhaps bashfulness—creasing her face. "Mr. Jaager, I did not expect you home so early."

"So you thought you could just come 'round and snoop?"

She glanced away. "I'm interested in your off-the-grid energy systems."

Paris blew out a scoff. "Interested in how they can be converted to shale oil?"

Madison blushed. "I understand this must seem highly irregular—"

"Highly," Kace agreed.

She gaped, her gaze darting between the two of them. "I…I thought my engineers could benefit from knowing about alternative energy sources."

Paris stepped forward. "What the hell for?"

Kace grabbed her elbow in warning.

"That's a fascinating thought, Ms. Danes." He drew in a breath in a vain attempt to calm himself. "Well, I'm home now and can answer any questions. I can show you the storage system and power monitors, if you like."

Madison glanced at Paris, a little crinkle of what looked like fear marring her forehead. "I think I should just go. I have enough information I can work with."

She gripped her notebook and cell phone and climbed back into her car. She drove off smoothly, almost casually, like she didn't care.

Or was trying to convey a façade of not caring.

"*Die Hard.* We're watching fucking *Die Hard.*"

Kace chuckled at Paris's pronouncement. "Let's get the popcorn started."

Madison rested her head against the edge of the whirlpool bathtub in the Bailey's bridal suite. Her cell phone lay on the granite tub deck, just within arm's reach.

She really shouldn't contact him. No, she shouldn't.

But she needed to explain herself. Apologize even.

Kace deserved that much.

Moments later the cell phone was in her hand and she was searching for his contact entry, cleverly disguised as Foxy Ranger.

Sorry about earlier today.

She waited, staring up at the ceiling, apprehension still rattling her nerves despite the soothing jets of water.

A beep splintered the silence. She closed her eyes and braced herself before picking up her phone.

What the hell were you thinking?

She probably deserved that. Okay. She absolutely deserved that. And Kace deserved an answer.

Look, I have an idea. I think it's a great compromise. Something you and the mining industry can live with.

I don't think you understand. I can't live with this deal at all. No matter how you sugarcoat it.

A slow inhalation calmed her nerves. *Kace, this project is going through whether you want it to or not. It'll get fast-tracked once it passes the House. But I can stall it while I get my Board of Directors to agree to this compromise.*

What is this supposed compromise?

He was obviously annoyed. She couldn't blame him. *I can't tell you yet.*

She imagined him sighing heavily, rolling his eyes. *And if they don't agree?*

That couldn't happen. They'd have to. *Just wait. They'll agree. If it's any consolation, my plan will cause a delay in construction, and, well, with all the politics going on today, who knows how long that delay might last?*

The beat of silence was a tad too long.

OK. Can't wait to see what your brilliant plan is. Snark oozed from every word.

She'd show him. Well, first she'd have to convince the board.

Madison set the phone down, her body no longer mired in dread but charged with possibility.

KACE LEANED AGAINST the kitchen counter and tossed the phone onto the table. It buzzed in complaint.

He was done with Madison, really he was.

Another buzz.

Fuck.

He picked up his phone.

Bettina.

I'm sending a formal email to your work address, but just a head's up: I found your evidence.

Kace's heart skipped a beat. *Evidence?*

A letter from a former slave who made her way to San Francisco. She was one of the escaped slaves who sheltered at Fort America.

"Holy fuck," he muttered out loud.

His heart pounded. *This is beyond amazing.*

I know! Check your email tomorrow. I'll attach photos and transcriptions. We have to get them to stop the mining project. I'm contacting everyone I know—plus the press. Call everyone you know. Post on social media. We have evidence now. We need to step up the archaeological digs. Make Fort America a protected site.

Hope invigorated him. *I'll do what I can, Bett. Thanks for pursuing this.*

An excited smiley face began the response. *Of course I'm pursuing this. It's my heritage!*

Black America's heritage.

Fort America's heritage.

America's heritage.

CHAPTER TEN

Los Angeles

Madison slunk down in the burgundy leatherette booth in the back of the bar at Mariano's, Dad's favorite Los Angeles restaurant. He wasn't often in L.A., especially since her divorce, but there was some sort of engineering conference in town he'd made the excuse of going to. She'd arrived at Mariano's early purposely to get at least one drink in her without Dad's usual disparaging comments about calories and the prying eyes of the press. Although any member of the press choosing to dine at the stodgy restaurant was probably way too old to know who she was anyway.

Arriving early also meant Dad couldn't order for her. She'd already instructed the waiter to bring her their famous ravioli, and ignore whatever Dad said. She'd tipped the waiter handsomely and asked him to warn her—well, she'd said "let her know"—when Dad had been seated. She'd wait until he'd ordered his martini, giving her a chance to down her second manhattan and check her lipstick in the ladies' room.

A group of boisterous men—white, late middle-aged, wearing suits—padded down the dark patterned carpet of the dim bar. Too many uncomfortable moments with Dad's friends taught her to ignore men like these, to not give them any reason to notice her. She remained still, staring at her cell phone.

They stopped without so much as a glance in her direction and sat in the neighboring booth.

Crude jokes followed by suggestive chuckles wafted in the air. She quietly slid deeper into the corner.

"I'm serious, just get a woman to front the whole operation. They don't know a thing about money but the press loves touting how women are making achievements."

Madison could practically hear the air quotes around "achievements".

"Not to mention the benefit of getting to look at short skirts and high heels."

Chuckles all around.

"Even better if it's a family member. Daughter, sister, wife."

"Yeah, like Danes."

A shiver ran up Madison's spine raising every hair on her head.

"Woo-ee, his daughter is one hot piece of ass."

"I'd like to get some of that."

She should be disgusted. Okay, she was. But she was also intrigued. Always prepared for moments like this, Madison surreptitiously slid on her sunglasses.

"Madison Danes is not some dumb blond—"

She discreetly wrapped a scarf around her hair.

"Which makes her dangerous."

More chuckles all around.

"Yeah, but I bet she doesn't know what Duke Danes has done with Danergy."

Oh, please, do tell.

"What she doesn't know is Danes holds the power. He's pretending she has it, but he's drawn up paperwork that I bet she hasn't seen. He said it just makes it easier to have a woman heading things up, especially in his line of business. Libtards think fracking is evil. A woman at the helm softens the blow. They're non-threatening. Once the project begins, believe me, Duke will throw her out."

Dad? Throw her out? Madison's vision blurred as anger boiled within. So Dad didn't trust her, didn't believe in her, didn't care about her—

No. Wait. Of course he did. Why was she even listening to these jackasses?

She took a hefty swallow of her drink. *Hell.* She downed the rest of it.

Because deep down she always knew something was not quite right about her presence at Danergy. She was L.A., while the company was Texas all the way. She'd been married to a movie star for a decade. Never got an engineering degree. There were plenty of guys at the firm who knew way more shit than she did.

The waiter in her pay approached. Except for a fleeting acknowledgment of her new attempt at being incognito, his expression remained impassive.

"The gentleman has arrived," he said quietly.

"Have a manhattan sent to our table. Extra cherry."

The waiter nodded with a suppressed smile.

Madison took her time in the ladies room before joining Dad.

He waved at her drink as she took her seat.

"I told him you didn't drink that stuff. That you only drank wine."

"Thanks, Dad. But I do drink that stuff."

Dad raised his martini in her direction, a new crease forming between his brows. "Cheers, then."

They clinked glasses and Madison took a sip. Then another.

"So what did you want to discuss, Maddie?" Dad slid the menu to the edge of the table.

Besides you using me as a shill? "I have some ideas for the Fort America project."

"Oh?" Dad looked away to smile at the waiter, then gave his—and Madison's—order.

The waiter nodded, with a reassuring glance Madison's way.

"Yes, I was thinking we should have an interpretive center in Freegate, the town nearby."

"What the hell is an interpretive center?"

"You know, like at museums, with displays explaining what hydraulic fracturing is and the history of energy and mining. Perhaps a bit about the geology and natural resources of Fort America. Why it's a robust environment for energy extraction. Something more elaborate than the small exhibit in the lobby of the luxury hotel you said we should have."

Dad grunted.

Madison fished out a cherry in her manhattan. She chewed casually. "And I really think Danergy's operation in Fort America should be run partly on renewables."

"Renewables?" He scowled. "What do you mean?"

She downed the rest of her cocktail. "You know, solar panels, wind turbines, possibly geothermal."

Dad crimsoned. "Why the fuck would we want to do that?"

Madison smiled the saccharine smile she reserved for annoying clients. "It makes us look good." *Like having a woman at the helm.*

"Maddie," there was that condescending tone again, "the local electric company is not going to be happy about that. And the politicians supporting us need the electric company's donations to run their campaigns. The next election is going to be a doozy what with all the coloreds—"

Jesus. Coloreds? What the fuck? Who even says that?

"And the gays—"

Well, he could have said something worse.

"And the—"

Dad stopped. He glanced away before turning his frown on his half-drunk martini.

"Who else, Dad?" Madison buttressed herself. "The women?"

He thinned his lips. "All those damned women who marched because they want abortions and free love."

And equal rights.

A plate of veal scallopini was set before Dad. A gorgeous bowl of ravioli in tomato sauce was set before Madison. She immediately speared a perfect piece of ravioli and blew cool air on it.

Dad gaped briefly before stabbing his meat.

For an old-school Italian joint, Mariano's got ravioli better than any chichi spot in West Hollywood.

"Dad, I'm talking about compromise. Get the Democrats on board with the project by offering solar power and stuff."

He kept his focus on his plate. "We don't need 'em."

Madison ate. She'd only ever had a taste of Mariano's ravioli, and now, here was a whole plate before her. She was not going to let Dad's sour mood spoil her lunch.

"Maddie, everything's ready to go. You don't need to sweeten the deal for anybody. We have enough representatives on our side to proceed. Don't worry your pretty little head."

"All right, Dad. I just thought I'd throw the idea out there, in case you needed it."

Madison enjoyed her meal all the while her pretty little blond head plotted her next move.

*****

Fort America

IT WAS A POWERFUL STORY, to be sure. And, with her charismatic enthusiasm, Bettina was the perfect ambassador to the past.

Kace had set up—with the help of Paris, of course—a press conference to reveal the contents of the letter Bettina had found. Major media outlets had been invited, as well as specialty journalists and bloggers. Plus, the local congressional representative, Christine Davis, would be in attendance.

Because of Fort America's remoteness, all of this was to take place via video conference. Except that Bettina and the representative would actually be present at Fort America.

"So this is where you work."

Bettina seemed a little impressed—or maybe just surprised—the visitor center in such a remote location was housed in a permanent building rather than a portable structure.

"Yeah."

"Not bad." Bettina smiled. "I guess you'll do fine once I'm retired."

Kace chuckled. "It's *your* staff I'm worried about. What'll they do without their fearless leader?"

Paris approached a bit tentatively, clearly in awe of the older ranger. "I set up this corner of the center for the conference, Supervisor Yeager," she said.

A backdrop with old Fort America promotional posters and a map of the area was hung behind a table with a microphone and three chairs.

"Thank you, Paris." Bettina reached into her briefcase. "I have these facsimiles of the letter in case you want to zoom in on them."

Dennis entered carrying a video camera. He tipped his hat to Bettina. "I've got some good footage of the landmarks. B-roll, as they say in the biz." He winked at Paris.

Finally glad to put her film degree to use at work, Paris had plotted the details of the whole endeavor. They would hold the press conference, tape it, then she would edit the video with cutaway shots of Fort America and the letter. The finished video would be posted on the park's YouTube channel—which wasn't used as much as it should be. Links to and excerpts from the video would also be posted on official social media, then the Rogues would pick it up with the intention of making it go viral.

"Kace, come here," Paris directed.

He stood before her as she checked his collar and tie, something he had gotten used to since he hired her. Paris was all about making sure Kace was presentable when it was important.

"Show me your teeth."

"Yes, mother." He offered a toothy grin.

"Good. No kale." She gave him the once over. "Damn that uniform looks good on you. As if you got it tailored while you were in—" She rolled her eyes. "Shit, Kace. She didn't."

"She did. And it's none of your business."

"It's like accepting favors," she whispered.

"Not when she holds all the power."

Paris sighed heavily. "Okay, yeah, I guess."

His chest tightened with the reminder of his time with Madison. He'd have to put it all behind him, though. This video was their last ditch effort to upset Danergy's plans to destroy Fort America.

His office phone rang. Paris ran to pick it up.

Dennis proceeded to check a camera on a tripod aimed at the table with the microphone. "Kace, I thought we could try it with you standing instead of sitting at the table. It might work better to zoom in and out, rather than pan across." He indicated a spot in front of the table. "Can you stand right there please?"

Paris sauntered in, crestfallen. "Christine Davis says she can't make it. She offered to read her prepared statement via Skype, however." Paris glanced between Kace and Bettina. "I think it's important to have that official stamp of approval."

"How about I set up a laptop at the table where our representative would have sat," Dennis suggested as he glanced around like a director mired in thought. He grinned. "This could be good. Emphasizes how remote Fort America really is. How it was a good place for slaves to hide."

Bettina chuckled.

"Sounds like a plan," said Paris. "Thanks, Dennis. Nice to know we have lots of troops in this fight." She clapped her hands. "All right, everyone. Let's get this party started."

Orange County, California

LUCKILY FOR MADISON the House was on break and representatives were back at their home offices. Last thing she wanted was to go back to the heat of Washington, D.C. Meeting with Congresswoman Wendy Morton at her Orange County office was much more preferable.

Wendy had been instrumental in garnering momentum for S.3806. When Madison had first approached her about legislation, Wendy had said a bill to develop energy resources in Fort America would have a better chance of passing if it started in the more business-friendly Senate. Wendy had worked with senators to draft the legislation and gather cosponsors. Now that the bill had passed and had moved on to the House, she was spearheading efforts to garner support among her fellow representatives.

Madison dropped her purse on the visitor chair and paced behind it.

Wendy sat at her desk, watching. "What's wrong, Madison?"

"I need you to pull the plug on the Senate bill. Not let the House approve it."

"*What?* Are you serious?"

"I am."

Wendy drew in a long inhalation as she flexed her hands on top of her desk. "Madison, I—and you—have put a lot of effort into this project. It'll be a lot of work to un-convince people now that we've convinced them, unless we start offering favors we might not be comfortable with. Plus, I can't guarantee any support for future legislation if *certain* energy lobbyists—" she narrowed her eyes at Madison, "are perceived to be wishy-washy."

Shit. She hadn't thought this through.

Wendy indicated Madison should sit. "Something's up. Why this sudden change of heart?"

"It's my father." Madison took a moment to calm her roiling emotions. "Turns out he's only using me as a false front. He has no intention of letting me call the shots at Fort America. And I need to call the shots. I want this project to go through as smoothly as possible. But if I can't be at the helm, if this is not *my* project, then I don't want the deal to go down."

"Ah." Wendy nodded with a snort of understanding. "Well, the best we can do is call the representatives we courted and tell them the deal is not as important as once thought, and suggest they vote their conscience."

"Shit." This time Madison said it out loud.

"Madison, I can't re-lobby everyone to change their vote unless there's something stronger than the fact that Duke Danes is a deceitful father."

"Yeah, I see that now."

"Tell me what happened."

Madison stopped pacing and sat. "I told Dad my ideas and was immediately shot down along with 'don't worry your pretty little head'."

Wendy scoffed with understanding. "What did he find objectionable?"

"I had this apparently radical idea to integrate renewables as a source of power for the fracturing operation. A sort of concession to environmentalists that we're not intent on destroying the earth."

A beat of silence was the only indication of Wendy's surprise. "Well, the best I can offer is what I just said: Let the House vote their conscience and at least we'll have not quite the mandate we were originally hoping for. That way we won't appear so victorious."

Madison grunted in acquiescence. A soft knock on the door pulled her out of her funk.

"Come," Wendy directed.

A pretty golden-brown haired young woman stepped through the door. "Ms. Morton?"

"Yes, Jessica?"

"Pardon me, but you had said you wanted me to alert you if there were any developments to the Fort America situation?"

Wendy glanced at Madison with a raised brow. "Yes?"

How fortuitous. Or unfortunate.

Jessica shot a star-struck glimpse Madison's way. "There's been a press conference, ma'am. About some discovery at the fort. A letter, I think."

"How interesting," Wendy said genuinely. "When did this happen?"

"I just heard about it on social media. The presser happened a few days ago. I have the laptop loaded with a video the Park Service posted on YouTube."

Jessica set up the laptop on Wendy's desk with tentative movements, perhaps a touch of nervousness.

"Thank you, Jessica."

With a nod and a smile aimed at Madison, Jessica exited.

Wendy started the video. It began with shots of the fort-like rock formations, then the interior of the visitor center, while a woman's voice narrated a brief history of Fort America.

"*...besides the natural beauty of the site, Fort America is important because of its history. Over one hundred and fifty years ago, escaped slaves, guided by Native Americans, found refuge at the top of the highest plateau...*"

Madison couldn't listen. She didn't need to be reminded of what Danergy planned to despoil.

Suddenly, there was a close-up of the park's superintendent.

Oh my God. Kace looked good. Too good.

Madison's cheeks burned. She fought to keep her breathing even, and hoped Wendy didn't notice.

"Handsome devil, isn't he," muttered Wendy. "Are all our National Park Service rangers that hot?"

Madison swallowed the drool pooling in her mouth before offering a dull chuckle. "I certainly hope so."

He was gorgeous in his tailored suit, crisp shirt, and perfect tie, looking every bit as delectable as she had remembered and had continued to fantasize about. If only she could tell him everything had changed, and she was trying to stop the project.

He wouldn't care. Wouldn't believe her until she'd been successful. And success was definitely not assured.

Kace was poised and comfortable before the camera—quite a change from the hearing. He introduced Christine Davis, a congressional representative in whose district the park was situated. The camera focused on a laptop with the image of the legislator phoning it in.

"Oh," said Wendy. "That's Chris. I'd almost forgotten she's got part of Fort America."

Chris said a few words about the importance of preserving America's historical parks and natural resources as they *were* America, typical promotional blather said by every politician with a National Park in their district.

Whatever Kace was trying to achieve with this stunt was not working in the first five minutes.

The camera panned back to Kace. Okay, so maybe the stunt would work with cutaways to the handsome silver-fox ranger every once in a while.

"The history of Fort America has always included the legend of a group of escaped slaves hiding from those in pursuit, attempting to re-enslave them. But, unfortunately, there has been no hard proof that this event ever occurred." His expression brightened. "Until now."

Madison gaped. She glanced at Wendy who mirrored her expression.

"I would like to introduce Bettina Yeager, Superintendent of the San Francisco National Historic Park. After years of research and sleuthing she has made an amazing discovery."

Kace moved from his position in front of the table on which the now-closed laptop sat, and took a seat next to an older African-American woman. Kace and Ms. Yeager shook hands. A warmth exuded between the two, the warmth of friendship, respect, and affection.

Ms. Yeager was clearly part of Kace's world, a world where power and influence did not matter, but instead simple existence, a shared history, the joy of friendship, and the struggle of day-to-day living.

A twinge of envy burbled within. Would Madison ever stop wanting to be part of his life?

"This is incredible."

Wendy's interjection made Madison focus on the video. Ms. Yeager was speaking, indicating two pieces of paper laid out before her on the table.

"For my own study on African-Americans in the Pacific maritime industries, I spent years combing archive after archive, hoping to find a document, a letter, a journal entry, anything that was pertinent to my research. In the course of this research, I discovered something of possible interest housed at the Women's Rights National Historical Park in New York. That discovery led me to another housed at the National Archives in Washington, D.C. This letter," Ms. Yeager pointed to one of the pieces of paper, "was buried in the papers of the Women's Loyal National League."

The camera zoomed in on the letter, the handwriting feminine and flourished, while Ms. Yeager continued to speak.

"A woman named Ruth wrote to members of the Women's Loyal National League thanking them for providing her with the names and connections of allies on the West Coast of the United States. In the letter, Ruth recounted her journey with seven other escaped slaves, describing landmarks we recognize today, including Fort America."

The video cut to a map of how the park was situated within the larger Southwestern United States and northern Mexico area.

"Ruth had heard there was freedom in Mexico. That she could get to Mexico through Texas. In fact, many slaves had trod the Freedom Trail to Mexico."

A graphic showed a map of two routes from the southern United States through Texas to Mexico.

Incredible.

Wendy gasped. "I never knew about this."

"Neither did I." Madison shook her head.

Ms. Yeager continued. "Ruth found herself, along with several other slaves, part of a cattle drive in the panhandle of Texas. With the help of local *Tejanos*—Texans of Mexican descent—the slaves decided to take a chance to freedom."

A graphic depicted the assumed path of the slaves, which was quite a bit off from the usual trajectory to Mexico.

"The now fugitive slaves had hoped to meet up with the Santa Fe Trail, and continued west to find it. All along they were pursued by slavers seeking to recapture them. And, as we now know, they were slowed down a little because Ruth was pregnant."

Madison's heart skipped a beat. Could it get any better? She smiled. If Kace was involved, then probably.

"In her letter, Ruth writes they struggled to keep their distance from the slavers, until a group of Southwest Native Americans led them to a dry and rocky place high up a hill on a plateau. She describes the climb to the top, how from the valley below their destination resembled a castle from a picture book she used to show her master's children."

The video cut away to a canonical image of the crenellations topping Fort America as seen from the ground.

"Ruth and the others hid on the plateau for several weeks while the Native Americans distracted and frightened off the slavers."

Next was a shot of the desolate plateau at the top of Fort America, a magnificent view in the background.

"But the miscalculated route to Mexico which instead sent the fugitives west, had taken longer than expected. During Ruth's time on the Fort America plateau she gave birth to a daughter, the child of a man named Roland, one of the other escaped slaves who had secretly been her lover. The birth of the child had delayed the flight to freedom, but the others had refused to leave Ruth and Roland alone."

The next shot was a sepia-toned photograph of a young African-American woman wearing a Victorian dress, standing poised and elegant amid typical portrait studio props.

"The couple named their daughter Liberty."

A chill stung Madison's flesh. Wendy wiped the corner of an eye.

Ms. Yeager picked up the letter. "Let me read to you what Ruth wrote: *We did not have a proper surname when we left the Natives' encampment. We came upon a cattle man on horseback, his skin as black as ours. He lived as a free man. He had the name Maundy Gowdy, so we took his last name as our own.*"

The video showed a map of the western United States.

"Upon arriving in California, members of the group went their separate ways. Ruth, Roland, and Liberty Gowdy traveled to San

Francisco. Ruth explains in her letter they're headed up to Oregon or maybe Washington as Roland hopes to get a job in shipping or logging."

Ms. Yeager looked straight at the camera with a faint smile, perhaps of triumph. "This is a story of America through and through. African Americans escaping the horrors of slavery. Mexican Americans and Native Americans helping them. A child born in freedom. The desire to go forward and prosper on one's own merits. The quintessential American Dream. This is Fort America's story. I hope all Americans can work together to preserve this historic, iconic, and majestic place."

Jesus. Kace had just raised the stakes.

Wendy blew out a loud sigh. She called for Jessica, who came in promptly.

"You said you found this on social media? How?"

"You asked me to follow all the Rogue accounts," Jessica said almost apologetically. "There's a trending hashtag 'Save Fort America'. And, if you look, the video has, like, a million views."

Not quite. But almost. *Holy fuck,* almost.

"Thank you, Jessica." The young woman exited once again.

Wendy offered a crooked smile. "Madison, *this* is something I can work with. But only if you really are serious about stopping the Danergy project."

"I am."

"All right. Let's get to work."

CHAPTER ELEVEN

Los Angeles

Madison leaned her elbows on the breakfast bar in her kitchen and stared at her laptop. The spreadsheet did not lie. She had a fuck-ton of work to do for the new legislation. Wendy did, as well. *She* still had to write the bill and get cosponsors before she could introduce it in the House. Madison, as a lobbyist, just had a lot of glad-handing ahead of her.

A lot of glad-handing.

And a lot of apologizing to all the politicians she'd lobbied not too long ago to get them on board with the previous legislation to allow mining at Fort America. The new bill would protect Fort America from energy development, but also, if passed, negate S.3806 which was now in the House. The hope was S.3806 would not even be considered by the House, and would, therefore, die.

But would legislators change their minds? She could only hope.

The Women's March and Black Lives Matter had brought issues surrounding those movements to the fore of the American political landscape. And now they had the perfect intersection of histories: African Americans escaping slavery; a pregnant woman giving birth to a daughter she named Liberty; Native Americans and Mexican Americans helping the fugitives toward freedom.

The ultra-right and traditionalists would remain hold-outs. But surely representatives not in the pocket of the energy industry could be swayed to vote for the new legislation? Plus, there was fear of a "Blue Wave" ousting conservatives in the upcoming election. Perhaps representatives would see the utility of catering to their more liberal constituencies. Or decide to embrace an "America for all" narrative.

The cells of Madison's spreadsheet began to merge together. She blinked, exerting effort to focus on the task at hand. Their strategy this time around had changed completely. Wendy would contact a couple of members of the Congressional Black Caucus she knew personally, and ask them to cosponsor the new bill. Madison would contact a couple of the more feminist of the conservative women in Congress, asking them to take the lead with the Congressional Caucus for Women's Issues and help bridge the gap with conservative men.

Madison snorted. Men of her father's ilk would not be persuadable.

But men like Kace—

She shook her head to rid herself of prurient thoughts nowadays seemingly always at the ready. It was not about *him*. No. It was about *her*. About making a statement against the chauvinism of her father's generation.

A deep breath helped center her. A line on her spreadsheet— in green—indicated how they were to approach the more liberal members of Congress. She and Wendy had hammered out some talking points: that there was new information in the Fort America situation, and while voting for this new measure might not stop or prevent fracking in all of America's National Parks, such a move would at least kill this specific project. Legislation to protect all National Parks from any future development would have to wait for another day. Putting this current project on hold was a good start.

Madison saved her spreadsheet and closed her laptop. Dad would be spitting mad, but Kace…

Shit. She should not be thinking of him right now.

Still, he'd be pleased with this turn of events. But she'd wait to tell him her role in the matter after all the cheering had died down.

Fort America

KACE STARED at the special delivery letter, anger and disbelief blurring the words on the page.

He was being relocated. After over a decade at Fort America, the Secretary of the Interior had decided Kace would best serve the National Park Service at an urban park in the middle of a small town across the country.

Why?

Because "his goals and values for the development of America's natural landscape are not in line with the goals and values of the Secretary and the current administration". The new appointment would give Kace "the opportunity to exhibit his loyalty in a less distracting environment".

The video. It had to have been because of the video. He slumped back, his office chair squeaking underneath him.

He'd heard about forced relocations and "recommended" early retirements of Parks superintendents ever since the most recent Secretary of the Interior had been appointed. In this new Department of the Interior loyalty was expected, but not to the

United States of America. No. Loyalty was to the current administration occupying the executive branch of government.

His patriotism was being called into question. *His.* A soldier and public servant who had served his country for almost forty years.

Damn it.

If given the chance to do it over, he'd still have made that video. Because he was loyal to the idea of liberty in a free democracy, loyal to his country, loyal to those in the past who had made the United States a great country, and loyal to Americans today who deserved to know their history.

Kace exhaled his frustration. He had a month. A fucking month to pack and get his ass across the country.

A crisp knock on his office door was directly followed by Paris's entry.

"Hey Kace, Dennis and I—" She stopped and stared at him, cheerfulness swiftly morphing into concern. "You okay?"

He handed her the letter.

She read it. "Holy fuck." She shook her head. "Fuck, this is my fault. The video—"

"Was one of the best things we've ever done."

Paris plunked down in the chair on the other side of the desk. "You're not the first super this has happened to."

"I know."

"We haven't been successful in stopping a relocation. You know, the Rogues. We do our best though."

"I know," Kace admitted. "But you try. And you raise awareness of the situation."

"Best we can do is get the word out and link it to the other purges. Besides the Rogues, I'll contact a few journalist friends. I've made some friends in high places, what with all the attacks on the press these days."

"I really appreciate this, Paris."

"I can't believe this is happening to us."

Us. Because Fort America was a family.

She stared at the letter. "Can I make a copy of this?"

"The photocopy machine is down the hall. I believe it has a scanning function as well."

Paris chortled. "Dennis insisted on it. Now I see how useful it can be." She grabbed the envelope. "We got your back boss. Don't despair."

Hope stretched Kace's mouth into a diffident smile.

Los Angeles

THE TV BUZZED in the background as Madison gazed out her living room window. The lights of Los Angeles twinkled and changed color while traffic ebbed and flowed.

She clinked the ice in her manhattan-on-the-rocks. Doing what she had just done had made her feel more alive than being CEO of Danergy. She sipped her drink, the rye whiskey strong and delicious on her tongue.

Behind her, the newscast jingle blared. "*When we return, fallout at Fort America as a recent video prompts a forced resignation.*"

Madison froze, drink poised before her mouth. She moved to the couch to perch on the edge.

The commercials were interminable. When the newscast returned, her heart clenched. The photo in the upper right was of Fort America's iconic crenellation.

"*Fort America is one of the country's least known National Parks, and yet it has been making more news than Yosemite this week. Kara Seaton has the story.*"

Ms. Seaton looked very serious as she delivered her introduction. Very serious.

C'mon, c'mon, get to the meat of it.

"*...after the park produced a video of a recent discovery verifying a brief occupation by escaped slaves, the Department of the Interior got involved.*"

The story cutaway to a spokesman from the Interior Department. "The Secretary of the Interior feels such an important discovery should have been brought to his attention first, before being broadcast carelessly."

Huh. Secretaries of the Interior never got involved at such a micro level.

"*The incident prompted the reassignment of Fort America's superintendent Kace Jaager.*"

A prickling chill surged over her. *What?*

And there he was, handsome as always but looking a bit unnerved as he spoke into a reporter's microphone.

"I've served the National Park Service for decades, and thought I had found a home here at Fort America, so, yes, I am profoundly sad to have to leave." His lips tightened, the sign he was steadying his emotions.

The newscast cut back to the Interior spokesman. "The Secretary feels it is his prerogative to match superintendents with the best location for their skills," he said ingenuously.

Wow. Really? This was bald-faced doublespeak.

"The Secretary is certain Keys Jaager—"

Kace, you jackass.

"—will be more at home in an urban setting."

The photo of Kace holding a cuneiform tablet during the Gulf War popped up on the screen. "An archaeological specialist in the army during Operation Desert Storm," Ms. Seaton narrated, "Dr. Jaager has spent his tenure at Fort America developing archaeological programs researching the history and legends surrounding the park."

Cutting back to the present, the camera focused on a park ranger, an older woman with a long gray braid. *Becky.* She had once admired Madison's jewelry.

"Kace is a wonderful boss and a fantastic ranger. He's reached out to schools to bring in disadvantaged kids to give them an experience in nature." Becky's laugh held a bittersweet edge. "The kids love their Ranger Kace."

Shit. The kids. They really did love their Ranger Kace. He'd changed their lives for the better.

"—Fort America just won't be the same without him." The young woman in a Park Service uniform was teary eyed. *Paris*.

Jesus, the poor girl looked devastated.

Madison downed her manhattan. If all her money and power and connections could do just a little bit of good, now was the time.

She had to save Kace's job.

She turned off the TV, poured another drink, and went to her office to strategize.

Fort America

CONCENTRATING ON WORK during the day was difficult knowing boxes were waiting to be filled when Kace got home. Working all day and packing most of the night was exhausting, physically and mentally.

Every night, Kace hit the sack utterly spent.

Paris had noticed. That afternoon she'd insisted he go home early so he could get a jump on packing and get a good night's sleep.

Kace stared at a stack of books. Why did he have so many books?

His scholarly bent was his downfall. If only he could stop analyzing and just follow orders mindlessly, like an automaton, he wouldn't have gotten himself into this mess. But no. He had to think like the doctor of philosophy he was.

He sighed and turned on the television. The news. *Great.* Like he needed a dose of depressing headlines.

"A letter-writing campaign to save the superintendent of a national park has been targeted at the Secretary of the Interior."

Jesus. Some other sorry-ass ranger was in his exact same predicament. They should form a club and have reunions.

"Current and former students of Bridget Mason Middle School have sent letters in support of Kace Jaager, the superintendent of Fort America National Park—"

Holy fuck.

"—who is being forced to relocate across the country."

Kace sat on the couch, which, thankfully, hadn't been packed up yet.

And there on the TV was Ingrid Brookes, one of the Teach For America field school counselors. "Ranger Kace has put his heart and soul into this program. He has made such a difference in the lives of these children."

Video of boisterous middle school kids followed. Some of them Kace recognized. He chuckled. They were always so enthusiastic.

"I love Ranger Kace." *Oh, jeez. Shawndell.* Such a fun kid. He was poised before the camera while behind him boys and girls made faces and waved. "He taught me about the history of my African-American heritage at Fort America."

"Dr. Jaager has been a force for good for so many children who come from underprivileged backgrounds," Ms. Brookes added.

A college-aged woman sat at a library table, open books strewn before her.

"Felicia Gonzales found her calling during one camping trip to Fort America," began the reporter's voice-over. *"From an economically disadvantaged background, she's now at UCLA studying environmental science."*

Jesus. She must have been in the program ten years ago.

"Ranger Kace exposed us to American history, geology, environmental issues, and what it means to be a public servant. I hope to follow in his footsteps."

A dull ache began to pound behind his eyes.

The newscast showed kids hand-writing letters on lined paper. *"Current and former students have written to the Secretary of the Interior asking him to not relocate Dr. Jaager. We were unable to get a response from the secretary's office about the letter-writing campaign."*

Ms. Brookes returned to the screen. "I hope Ranger Kace does not have to leave," she said. "He's irreplaceable."

He couldn't watch any more. He turned off the news.

Elbows on knees, Kace cradled his head. But the tears didn't fall. He was too numb to cry.

DESPITE KACE'S impending relocation, every day volunteers needed to be managed and decisions needed to be made. Plus, now that Fort America, and he as its superintendent, had some celebrity, Kace was obliged to make far more appearances in the visitor center.

Dennis came in from outside lugging the center's sandwich-board signs. A storm was brewing and staff had to batten down the hatches, as it were. In this case, make sure anything that could fall over or blow away was brought inside.

Kace grabbed one of the heavy wooden signs and helped Dennis lean them near the front door.

"Thanks, boss," said Dennis. "And I want to thank you for spending time out here with the volunteers. I know you have a lot to do, but I do appreciate you taking the time to talk to folks about the new research. I think it's important everyone knows the history of this place, and you tell the story so well."

Kace couldn't stop a smile, but he did stop the tears. "Thanks, Dennis."

Paris sidled up. "I've set up some boxes for your personal effects."

"Thanks, Paris." She'd been so good to him ever since they got the news of his reassignment. She'd offered to see if she could join him, tender her resignation, anything to make a statement.

"You're helping in ways beyond any typical government employee," he'd told her. "Plus you probably can't be part of the Rogues in a more tightly controlled urban setting. We need you fighting the good fight."

She'd reluctantly agreed.

"Jesus," hissed Paris. "Of all the gin joints…"

Kace followed Paris's gaze to the front door.

Madison.

"What the ever-loving fuck is she doing here?"

"Easy, Paris." Kace swallowed. "I'll handle this."

From her plaid button down shirt that hung untucked over a loose t-shirt, to her well-fitting but not too-tight jeans, Madison Danes looked like she belonged at a National Park.

She wore no make-up or, rather, it appeared as if she wore none. She strode forward on sturdy hiking boots, a fashionable backpack hanging on one shoulder.

"Mr. Jaager."

"Ms. Danes."

"May I speak to you in private?"

Paris stepped forward. Kace held out a hand as a warning.

"Please join me in my office," he said as calmly as he could.

Once inside the office, Madison stared at the assembled cardboard boxes. "Oh, wow. I guess I didn't expect to see that."

"DOI gave me a month. Have you ever had to move in a month?" He didn't bother hiding his annoyance.

She sucked in her lower lip. "No."

If she'd had, she probably had "people" who handled such matters.

"Did you hear about the letter writing campaign by the kids at Bridget Mason Middle School in L.A.?" Her voice was quiet, subdued.

He met her gaze, a crease in her forehead hinting at apprehension.

"I did. With all the media reports, how could I not? I sent a letter back to the school thanking everyone. I was deeply moved. I'm afraid their efforts were all for naught though, and they'll be sorely disappointed."

Madison unzipped her backpack and pulled out a file folder.

"I did a letter writing campaign of my own." She handed him the folder. "The Secretary of the Interior is a good friend of my father's. Our company has done a lot of favors for him. I mean before he was Secretary. He owes us this. Owes *me* this."

Kace eyed her before opening the folder. Inside was a letter on crisp white paper, the Department of the Interior seal embossed at the top, the signature at the bottom that of the secretary himself.

He read the few short paragraphs.

Jesus. Unbelievable.

The secretary wrote he had considered Ms. Danes' request to reinstate Kace and, in light of her comments, plus the several dozen letters received by school children and all the high-profile media attention, would grant it. The department would be issuing a statement presently once Dr. Jaager had been informed.

Of course this was what he wanted, wasn't it? So why was there a sour feeling in the pit of his stomach?

"What did you say to the Secretary?"

"Just that I would hate for the proposed project at Fort America to lose an individual so knowledgeable about energy and energy management."

"Um-hmm," he murmured. "Is that all?"

"Kace, there's growing opposition to Danergy doing anything at Fort America. The Secretary knows that. I think he only wants to fight one battle."

Okay. That made sense. Still, some piece of the puzzle was missing.

Holy shit.

"It was you, wasn't it? The letter-writing campaign involving the kids?"

Madison's cheeks turned a rosy red. "What do you mean?"

"Oh, c'mon, Madison. I doubt a bunch of teachers and kids even knew what was going on."

"Actually they did—" Her blush deepened.

"Ah-ha!"

"All right, I admit I instigated the letter-writing campaign. And organized the media attention on local and national news. I suspect there were a few more letters written after the broadcasts."

A knock on the door. "Come."

Paris entered holding a cardboard Priority Mail envelope. "This just came for you." She cast a disapproving glance at Madison.

Kace took the envelope. "Thanks." He nodded his dismissal at a scowling Paris.

The sender was none other than the Secretary of the Interior. Inside was a sealed envelope, and inside that was a letter on Department of the Interior stationery. The secretary thanked Kace for his service, and rescinded his order for Kace to relocate.

This was all too perfect. Kace met Madison's gaze. "What do you want from me?"

"What do I want…?" Madison gaped. "I just want you to do your job, Kace. Nothing more."

"All right. With pleasure."

"You don't seem very happy."

"Happy? The last week has been absolute hell. I'm still trying to make sense of all this. I mean I completely understand the secretary's motives. But yours? Not so much."

Madison grabbed a visitor chair and plopped down onto it. "I wanted you to get your job back because my father is a sexist jerk."

Okay. Now *that* was unexpected.

He paced for a moment before sitting in the other visitor chair, opposite Madison. He leaned forward. "You want to tell me?"

"I—" She looked away, her mouth pressed in a hard line. "Maybe not here," she said in a low voice, her gaze darting about.

Jesus. Was his office bugged? "Well, it's either here or—" he waved his hand to indicate his house—

And touched her knee.

An erotic thrill pulsed through him, an electric charge terminating at his crotch. Had she noticed? He glanced up at her.

Madison was flushed, her pupils wide.

Clearly their attraction had never waned.

She stood. "I'll bring dinner." Her voice was still low. "From the hotel. They have an excellent chef." She met his gaze, her expression reflecting the flustered desperation he felt. "Does five thirty work?"

"Yeah," he rumbled.

The door clicked shut after Madison left. Kace closed his eyes and dragged his hands across his face.

What the hell was he doing?

CHAPTER TWELVE

Madison parked in the driveway at Kace's next to his Jeep. She sucked in a long inhalation, a little of her trepidation releasing on the exhale. She was taking a risk. But, despite their differences, and the fact they were technically enemies, she trusted Kace more than anyone in her life at that moment.

Clouds had gathered from the afternoon's heavy winds, and now their billowing gray mass blocked the sun already sinking into the horizon.

Great. All she needed was a rain storm to make it seem like she planned to get stranded at a hot guy's house.

Curtains were drawn across the picture windows of the front room, giving the house a dull glow. She stood at the front porch, knuckles poised to knock.

Kace opened the door. He looked scrumptious in a tight sweatshirt and loose jeans, his hair perfectly mussed.

"Ah, dinner has arrived."

He took the insulated carry-out sack and bottle of wine. She untied and toed off her hiking boots.

"Wow. This smells good." He checked out the label on the wine bottle. "And this looks expensive."

She laughed and followed him into the kitchen.

Moving boxes, some open and waiting, others taped and labeled, were strewn about the living room. Furniture had been moved aside. The bookcase was half empty. In the kitchen, more boxes crowded the floor.

He pulled two plates from an almost-empty cupboard.

She plunked her purse on the counter. "Sit," she said indicating the kitchen table. "Just point me to some wine glasses and silverware."

"Glasses packed in the box by the refrigerator. Knives and forks still in that drawer there." He set the plates on the table.

She bustled around, giving herself a few moments to calm down before they would have to talk business.

"Why all the subterfuge? You just trying to get me alone?" His voice held an edginess.

She looked up from the box of glasses, pulled out two and placed them on the table.

"I'm here a couple of minutes and you're already flirting with me?" She uncorked the wine.

"Defense mechanism?"

He studied her a bit too intensely as she poured two glasses of pinot grigio. She sat and raised her glass. He clinked his rim against hers and took a gulp.

"Ten dollars down, only sixty left to go."

He chuckled briefly, then sobered. "You really think my office is bugged?"

"I don't know what to think anymore. When I heard about your being asked to leave, I was not entirely convinced it was just because of the video."

He stared into the depths of his glass. "I'm pretty sure it's just because of the video."

"Because…?" She studied his profile. "Members of your staff have been bad-mouthing higher ups?"

"Something like that."

"Hmm." She pulled dinner out of the bag placing each take-out box on the counter. She'd decided on comfort food, with an upscale twist. Penne pasta in a sauce of gruyere, cheddar, and blue cheeses with sausage medallions, plus Caesar salad and garlic bread. She set the table and arranged the dinner boxes in the center.

He helped himself, each scoop accompanied by animated mutters of approval. He shoveled pasta in his mouth and moaned. "Thanks. I needed fancy mac-n-cheese tonight."

Her forced smile must have given away her true emotions. He frowned.

"What's going on Madison?"

She sighed. "I had this brilliant idea. For Danergy, for this project. It really was brilliant." She piled pasta on her plate. "My father shot it down, and in the course of shooting it down, revealed he had no intention of actually letting me run the company he had put me in charge of." One bite of the penne revealed why Kace had moaned. The cheese sauce was divine. "Dad just needed a woman figurehead to give the company a feminine appeal. You know, to soften the blow of raping the earth."

Kace's mouth thinned into a line. "Shit. Sorry about that. That must have been a punch in the gut."

"Yeah. It was."

A blast of wind rattled the windows. A moment later, rain pounded on the roof. Kace continued to eat unaffected by the tumult outside. The storm, however, mirrored the disquietude within Madison.

"I think my power would have gone out right about now."

A glimmer of pride brightened his expression. "No power lines means no power outage. Plus, I have all those back-up systems in place. Not much sun today for my solar panels, but my windmill was able to pick up the slack."

"So the electricity isn't going to go out?"

His lips twisted into a smirk. "You sound almost disappointed. Should I break out the candles?" He winked.

Madison flushed. She hadn't thought this a romantic visit.

Or had she?

She grabbed her glass of wine and took a swig.

He chewed thoughtfully. "So, what was your brilliant idea?"

She made an effort to ignore the storm. "I wanted the fracturing operation to be partially run on renewables."

Kace paused, fork before his mouth. "Pardon?"

Madison laughed grimly. "Yeah, that's kind of what Dad said. Except not so politely."

"Okay, so let me get this straight." Kace put down his fork and stared at her. "You want to power *the* most destructive form of gas extraction with environmentally friendly energy?"

"Yes."

"The point being…?"

She sighed in exasperation. "The point being that, as an energy company, we embrace all forms of energy generation." She eyed him as she started on her salad. "Even hippie stuff like solar and wind power."

That made him chuckle.

"But Dad said no because why would we ever want to do such a thing?"

"Indeed." Kace's tone indicated he understood her sarcasm.

The low roar of thunder rumbled like an earthquake.

"Is this a regular occurrence in these parts?"

"Thunder storms?" Kace calmly dished out salad onto his plate. "Yeah. This time of year is our monsoon season."

Shit. And she was going to drive back to the hotel in this deluge?

"Anyway," she continued, "what Dad's forgotten is, while he may be able to sway the board to vote against me, he cannot control how I communicate to the public. I can still send out a press release stating what I plan to do as CEO."

"Meaning that you plan to run the plant on renewables?"

"Yeah." She stabbed at her salad. "I'm pissed my father set me up, got my hopes up as CEO, pretended I even mattered to him. If only there were something else I could do that would annoy the hell out of him."

Kace leaned back in his chair. "Well, you could say Danergy is no longer interested in fracking at Fort America. Or any National Park."

Madison stopped chewing and stared at him. He raised an eyebrow.

She swallowed. "I couldn't."

"But you're CEO, so you could."

She could. And, in a way, she was doing exactly that with the new legislation. She wanted to tell Kace about it, but it was too soon. Wendy didn't have all their cosponsors lined up yet.

"Kace, I know you'd like me to be all environmentalist, but this is really self-serving on my part. I'm pissed with my father. When the story of Ruth and Liberty came out…" Madison shook her head. "It was just too perfect. A letter written by a woman, a woman escaping enslavers who were probably all men…" She finished her salad. "I'm just tired of women being oppressed."

Kace downed his wine then replenished both their glasses.

"Besides, if I say Danergy's out, another company will step in. Like I said before, the renewables angle will help delay the project for who knows how long."

He narrowed his eyes. "Long enough for a change in government?"

"That's a distinct possibility."

He responded with a grunt.

Madison smiled. "There's dessert, you know."

Alarm flitted across his face.

She laughed. "It's not a come on. There really is dessert. A mini-apple galette. The hotel has a very good pastry chef."

"I sometimes get doughnuts there for my staff."

"Thus ensuring their loyalty."

Kace's chuckle was drowned out by a crack of thunder. Madison jumped. Kace smiled in sympathy.

"Our storms can get pretty fierce, but all the rain fills up my well, so I'm not complaining."

"I'm surprised your solar panels are still attached to your roof."

"Well, if a tree gets hit by lightning, branches or shards of trunk can potentially break a panel. We've created a perimeter to help prevent that occurrence."

Madison took their plates and set them by the sink. "That's amazing, really. I'm surprised more people don't live this way."

"Says the evil energy company executive."

She gave him a sneer as she casually leaned against the counter. "I'm serious. Why don't they?"

Kace got up and joined her at the sink. "Well, solar panels are expensive. There used to be more tax-based incentives and rebates, but a lot of that has gone by the wayside. And it doesn't benefit lower income folks at all. You need to have a pretty good income to get a tax credit and even be able to afford panels in the first place." He pulled two small plates from the cupboard. "In order to have a wind turbine, you need enough land. You might need permission from neighbors if it obstructs views. Geothermal is complicated and expensive. And, like I've said, maintaining an off-the-grid set up is a time suck and really only for energy nerds. Generally, if people live near power poles, they're fine with not having to think too much about power and where it comes from. They just want to plug stuff in."

"I guess you're right." Madison took the still-warm mini-galette out of the insulated bag. She cut it in half and put each piece on a plate and set them on the table. "Dessert is served *sans* knife and fork. You don't mind the informality, do you?"

"Not at all." He took a bite, a bit of apple jelly squooshing out at the corner of his mouth. His soft groan of satisfaction was a little too provocative. "This is delicious," he said as he composed himself while she contemplated licking the cinnamony goodness off his mouth.

"Have you thought about using your house as an example of alternative energy efficiency? I mean to tourists and such."

"Well, besides the fact I actually live here…" He trailed off for effect.

"Okay, yeah, I get that." She took another bite of the heavenly dessert. "But what about a demonstration building. Or even rigging up the visitor center?"

Kace shook his head. "You would not believe the amount of red tape we had to hurdle just to get the superintendent's house 'rigged up', as you say." He snorted before taking the last bite of his apple galette. "We convinced the Interior Department that, if worse came to worst, the superintendent could camp out with no electricity. But we couldn't put the visitor center at risk of being shut down."

Outside, the storm raged, thunder resounding in the distance. "Doesn't seem like your house is in danger of being shut down."

He grinned. "No, it doesn't, does it?"

Madison licked her fingers, savoring the last taste of the galette, averting her gaze from the other treat in the room.

Kace grabbed his wine glass. "Let's watch the storm." He indicated the living room with a nod of his head.

Madison followed him to the couch, snagging a corner before he set his wine glass down on the other side of the coffee table. He moved the TV table away from the picture windows.

"It's okay if I turn off the lights?"

A flush overcame her. "Sure," she said as nonchalantly as possible. Being alone in the dark with Kace was going to be a challenge.

He turned off the kitchen lights, then the lamp next to the couch, immersing them in the fading twilight growing into an eerie sort of darkness.

The sky had a glow to it, the moon and emerging stars trying to pierce the clouds and storm. Against the gray backdrop, trees danced in the wind. The silence in the living room enhanced the bluster of the wind, the scrape of shrubbery against the side of the house, the rain spattering the window, the thunder now in the distance. Madison relaxed into her corner of the couch.

Lightning lit up the view. The storm suddenly seemed oddly serene, the silence in the living room comfortable, as if she and Kace were long-time lovers who were meant to be together, not former lovers completely at odds.

Lovers? Such an old-fashioned term, but an apt one. How else could one describe their relationship?

Food, sex, and aggravation.

A clap of thunder jolted her to laugh in surprise.

Kace joined her with a chuckle. "Nice, isn't it?" He stood and walked to the window to look at the darkening scenery. "Sometimes I find storms almost spiritual."

Intriguing. "How so?"

"Man against Nature. Man working with Nature. We build a strong house. Nature fights back with a storm to humble us. We set up solar panels and wind turbines to harness and control Nature for our own needs. Nature responds with sufficient sunshine and wind. It's like symbiosis or, perhaps, more like synergy. Working together toward a greater good."

"Like what you do in your job."

He turned to her. "Pardon?"

"You know, as a public servant. Working with your team to benefit, well, America really. A greater good."

*****

AMERICA.

That's why he did what he did. He served America.

And she understood.

The emotion he'd been wanting to feel for days chose that moment to rear its ugly head.

Shit. No.

Not in front of her. He stared out the window, the storm a manifestation of the turmoil within.

No. No. No. No.

His eyes burned, tears pooling at the corners.

He drew in a long inhalation, struggling to steady the shudder in his lungs. He cleared his throat. "Thank you for getting my job back. You have no idea how much that means to me."

"I think I do," she said quietly.

Silence hung in the air, broken by the occasional sound of the storm raging outside.

"My work at Fort America is everything. It's my life."

Why the fuck did he just say that? The waterworks started, uncontrollable.

Kace leaned against the window jamb seeking support. Instead his legs gave way. He crumpled to the floor, the Persian rug softening his fall.

Madison got up from the couch and went to the kitchen. Probably needing more wine after watching him blubber like a baby.

She returned, sans wine, sitting cross-legged next to him. "Here."

She held out a handkerchief. He took it, the white square delicate and soft.

"What's this?"

"My attempt at being slightly more environmentally conscious."

Her initials *MD* were stitched in the corner in a swirly font. "Wow. You're serious."

"I am. You know, just trying to tone down my evil energy company executive reputation." She smoothed her hands over her thighs as she turned her attention to the window. "I believe I can accomplish more with compromise."

Kace's pulse calmed in a sudden wash of euphoria. Because of her closeness? "Sorry about your father."

An exasperated sigh was followed by a shake of her head. "I'm just mad he didn't even bother listening to me. I thought I had a good idea."

"An unusual idea."

"In this political climate, everyone tearing at each other's throats, it's important to show we can compromise."

"Like you getting my job back."

"No," she snapped. She exhaled heavily. "No, Kace," she said softly. "I did that for you. When I heard, I realized what a petty move it was on the part of the administration. It would serve no purpose, and destroy you." She met his gaze in the dark. "I knew it would destroy you."

"It did." *Shit.* His forehead ached as his eyes burned. He wiped the resulting tears with her handkerchief, the soft cotton reminding him of her empathy.

And that the last time they were together he had been the ultimate sexist pig.

"Madison, I'm indebted to you. I really am. And, honestly, I'm floored. The last time we were together..." He inhaled fortification. "Jeez, I acted like a caveman."

She snorted. "You did."

"I'm mortified."

"Don't be. I kinda liked it."

Emotion of a different sort pulsed through him, landing at his crotch. He wanted some physical contact, even to just hold her hand. But...

He couldn't. He shouldn't. She would have to make the first move.

The warmth of her hand enveloped his.

The exhaustion of sorrow fled his body, replaced by energetic need.

She leaned in and touched her lips to his in a delicate, whisper-soft kiss.

"Are you trying to seduce me, Ms. Danes?"

"I think so, Mr. Jaager."

"Was this your plan all along?"

Madison sat back. "No. Believe me it wasn't. Okay, well, there's always the lingering fantasy in the back of my mind."

Kace chuckled. "Yeah."

"I just…" She stared out the window. "Most men I know wouldn't have been comfortable with a woman getting their job back, much less being grateful for it."

"I'm not most men."

"Yeah. I know. And I need someone like you in my life. But that's impossible. It's like you're this prize dangling in front of me that I can never have."

"So I'm a prize, am I?"

"God, that was objectifying, wasn't it? Talk about mortification."

He laughed, then reached out his arm in invitation. She curled against him.

"This feels good. I think the last time I cried and laughed was watching some sappy movie with Paris."

"I envy her, you know. She gets to be with you every day. And you have a great rapport."

"*I* envy her, too. She's this new generation that just doesn't put up with shit. I'm too used to taking orders."

"I thought she was ex-army, as well?"

"Yeah, but imagine the kind of woman who goes into the army."

"One who kicks ass and doesn't put up with shit?"

"Ha!" He guffawed and gave her a squeeze. "You two are very much alike. Opposite ends of the political spectrum, but both very determined."

Madison stretched up to peck his cheek. "I'm pretty determined right now."

She stood and held out her hand. He stood and drew her into his arms. She melted into him, her curves fitting perfectly against his body as he took her in a luxuriating long kiss.

She broke off and tugged on the buttons of his fly. "Get naked." She trotted off to the kitchen.

He tore off his sweatshirt and tee, stripped off his jeans and briefs. He was fully nude when Madison returned to the living room.

She tossed a couple of condoms onto the couch.

"I guess you put some thought into this."

"Wishful thinking," she said with a wink.

A FLASH OF LIGHTNING highlighted Kace's gorgeous body. Madison placed a hand flat on his chiseled chest. She gave a little push.

"Sit."

He plopped onto the couch with a devious grin. His gaze never faltered as he rolled on a condom while watching her take off her jeans and panties.

"A lot easier to take off than those skin-tight ones you usually wear."

She glared at him. "You don't like my skin-tight jeans?"

"I never said that. But these new ones seem more practical, you know, for hiking. Or even just walking."

She shot him her best withering look as she slipped off her plaid shirt. She turned her back to him as she pulled off her t-shirt and unhooked her bra.

"Plaid's a new look for you, as well."

Holding her bra to her chest, she turned and faced him. "You're making fun of me."

"I've never seen you wear practical clothes before. Unless they were mine."

She slipped off her bra and laughed. "It's all part of my new environmentally friendly façade. You know, I may be an evil energy company executive, but I still hike and enjoy nature."

"Have you ever even hiked before in your life?"

She straddled him, playfully poking him in the chest. "Just up my mountains of money."

His eye roll quickly morphed into lust as she lowered herself onto his erection.

Oh, God, she'd missed this. Missed him. Missed his moaning. Missed his supple skin over hard muscles. Missed the way he thrust up as she slid down. Missed the way their movements echoed in perfect syncopation.

Lightning illuminated the desire twisting his expression.

She arced over him, claiming his mouth, his kiss. His palms burned hot under her shoulder blades, supporting her, holding her close.

A clap of thunder rumbled through her core.

He pressed his forehead against hers. "You should check out the view."

"I think I have a mighty fine view."

"There's a better one."

He grabbed her around the waist and, with a bit of a lurch, stood, still embedded inside her.

Jesus. Total primitive male move. And damned sexy.

He set her down right before the window, slipping from her body to leave her standing alone. He grabbed a kitchen chair and brought it over, swinging it around so the back was at the window.

He sat. Then pulled her on top to straddle him.

Before her was the most magnificent view of trees flailing in the wind, black branches dancing against a deep blue-purple sky.

She slid down his potency once again, closing her eyes briefly, concentrating on how wonderfully, how perfectly he filled her. She anchored a foot on the low window sill, leaving the other on the carpet, ensuring enough leverage to piston on his hard cock.

He held her at the waist as she took control of their pleasure.

The storm mirrored their passion. The wind matched their panting breaths, the rain their tears and sweat. Kace murmured sweet words against her skin before licking her breast and tugging her nipple into his mouth.

"Oh, God, Kace," she moaned, threading her hands in his hair.

He kissed his way across her chest to torment the other nipple.

She sighed. His gentle touch was freeing, relaxing, melting away her tension, the sensuality accompanied by the beauty of nature.

His world.

She could get used to this. Get used to him.

Unease shimmied up her spine. *No.* Getting used to him was the last thing she should do—

A bolt of pleasure shot through her, jerking her forward. Kace chuckled as he gripped more tightly then resumed grinding his thumb on her clit.

Kace took control now, thrusting into her so hard she had to grab his shoulders, tormenting her with his thumb, unstopping, relentless. She met his gaze to find determination mingled with ecstasy.

Madison let go, giving in to pleasure, to him, to a fantasy that would never be.

She came, gripping him, his groan of pleasure precipitating his orgasm. He wrapped his arms around her, his cheek pressed against her breasts as he murmured gratitude. She stroked his hair, her heart still thudding. Tears wet her lashes as reality slowly took hold.

Did she really have to give him up?

A CLEAR MORNING always greeted Kace after a major storm. And while a cloudless sky shone pale gold merging into the blue of day, his brain was mired in fog.

Madison lay next to him in his bed, on her stomach, one leg bent, arms akimbo. A vulnerable position that exposed her back—and her butt. Her gorgeous fleshy cheeks so inviting he wanted to kiss and suck until she was branded with his mark. Or spank her until she was pink and squirming.

Or take her from behind—

Jesus. What the hell was she doing to him?

Her unguarded pose implied she trusted him. The muffled snore of a sound sleeper implied a hell of a lot of trust.

Shit.

Madison was hot, great in bed, and they connected every time they got together. He could live like this, right? The occasional, surreptitious bang, usually following or followed by stupidly expensive gourmet food.

But she had no qualms about ravaging the earth, the landscape, the future. As much as she tried to sugarcoat Danergy's plan, she was going to destroy every fucking thing he believed in.

Would it be worth it?

CHAPTER THIRTEEN

Los Angeles

Madison stared through her office window at the lights of L.A. unfurled like a red carpet on an awards show. A scene a world away from the view beyond Kace's window. She loved cities, even seemingly boundless metropolises like Los Angeles. Cities had their own beauty—historic architecture, vibrant neighborhoods, ribbons of light illuminating dark streets.

But Kace had taught her an appreciation for the natural environment. That vast swaths of nature were a balance to, and a refuge from, the frenzy of city life. Their last night together had been a spectacular experience, revealing their passion as a glorious element of nature. Her orgasm had seemingly merged with nature itself.

She sipped her manhattan, the bitter-sweet cocktail sliding over her tongue languidly before burning down her throat.

Kace's life calling was protecting those swaths of nature purposely set aside for Americans to enjoy. A very noble calling indeed.

And what was her life's calling?

To be taken seriously as herself instead of as a rich guy's daughter or an actor's arm candy?

Jesus. How fucking self-serving.

She swirled her drink, the cherry bobbing gently in the crystal tumbler.

There was that night in D.C. where Kace had challenged her about her feminism. At the time she'd been annoyed. Just because she didn't follow radical tenets didn't make her any less of a feminist, just a different one. How long ago was that? It seemed like years, but was just, what? a couple months? not even?

So much had happened since.

And now, some of what he had been trying to convey to her was starting to make some sense.

"The patriarchy wants women to shut up and sit down in a corner."

Dad had been putting up road blocks through this whole process, had been making deals behind her back. He had never intended for her to be in charge.

"But if you're out of earshot, then they have no control over you, right?"

There were plenty of places to drill for oil and gas in the U.S., plenty of privately held land. There really was no need to defile pristine public lands. The whole point of even having National Parks was to preserve America's unique landscape for generations to come. The current administration was only looking to give a cheap deal to big donors. They certainly did not have the long term in mind.

While sleeping with the enemy, some of his leftist, liberal politics had clearly rubbed off on her.

Her laugh out loud almost spilled her drink.

She took a generous swig and leaned against the window jamb.

Was what she was about to do because she wanted to see Kace again with a clear conscience?

Maybe. But he was also right. And his idea for annoying the hell out of Dad was even better than hers. Plus, now that Wendy had her cosponsors and was just about to introduce legislation, the time was ripe.

Madison went to her desk and opened a new document on her laptop.

Press release, for immediate release…

In light of new information, Danergy Mining & Hydraulics is rescinding its interest to develop any land in Fort America. Furthermore, Danergy will lend support to any and all upcoming legislation to disallow fracking and mining on any United States public lands.

Danergy approves the action of the Secretary of the Interior of reinstating a fine public servant at Fort America…

Giddiness took hold as she hit *Send*. She swallowed a gulp of liquor then bit back a smile.

Dad won't see what's coming.

MY OFFICE. NOW.

Dad never texted in all caps. And never at six in the morning.

Okay, it was six her time, eight o'clock his time. And it was early afternoon in Texas by the time she arrived at Danergy headquarters.

The instant Madison stepped into Dad's office she knew he wasn't angry.

Nope. He was livid.

He paced behind his desk like a caged lion. "What the fuck did you think you were doing?"

Dad rarely used foul language with such caustic bitterness directed at her.

"Sending out a press release."

His lips tightened in a thin white line as his face turned crimson. "You are not allowed to put out a press release without the consent of the board."

"I've never heard that one. In fact, I seem to recall you've done the very same thing. Even after you retired as CEO of Danergy."

"That's different. I always had the full support of the board."

"After you cajoled them into seeing things your way."

A growl rumbled beneath his loud exhalation.

Madison drew in courage. "I'm CEO of Danergy now, Dad. I made the decision based on the new evidence. We have to honor this history, women's history, African-American history."

"No, we do not."

Another inhalation helped cool down her boiling blood. "And I say we do. For our image. I have decided that this company will do the right thing."

"The right thing is making money and not letting anyone get in our way. Like that damn park ranger."

Alarm skirred up Madison's spine. "Which park ranger, Dad?"

"The one who fought in Iraq." He waved a hand back and forth in the air. "The one at the hearing. Goddamn pesky protester. He was too much in the way."

Dad usually never cared about "pesky protesters". They were just background noise to his grand schemes.

"I told the Secretary of the Interior to get rid of him."

Alarm turned to anger.

"Someone must have had more pull with the Interior Department than I do."

"That someone was me, Dad."

"*You?*" His outrage was palpable. "*What the fuck?*"

The phone buzzed. Dad stared at her as he pressed the intercom button. "Yes?"

"Mr. Danes?" His secretary's drawl was so sweet and innocent. "You said you wanted to know when there was news on energy matters in Congress? Something's coming up on the news after the commercials. Channel Thirteen."

"Thank you, Darleen." He turned on the television. "Let's hope it's good news."

The female anchor of Channel Thirteen's afternoon report was poised and professional, as always. Behind her was an image of Fort America's crenellations.

Madison braced herself.

"*Moments ago, a bill to keep fracking out of Fort America was introduced in the House of Representatives.*"

She dared glanced at Dad who remained impassive. Only the tenseness in his shoulders revealed his true emotions.

The anchor had turned the report over to their Washington, D.C. field reporter.

"*...Representative Wendy Morton, a Republican from southern California introduced the bill.*"

Wendy appeared triumphant as she spoke into half a dozen microphones. "Due to the new evidence about an historic escaped slave presence at Fort America, the Congressional Black Caucus and the Congressional Caucus for Women's Issues feel any development projects in the area should be put on hold as evidence is gathered—"

Dad threw the remote against the wall, the device shattering into plastic shards. He turned to Madison, his hands balled into fists. "This is your doing."

"Dad, our project was going to face huge problems—"

"You called in favors, didn't you?"

"So what if I did? I learned that from you."

He raised his hands in the air, his fingers curling. "You did not learn how to sabotage and destroy your own goddamn business from me. You've just crushed our ability to pay our shareholders projected dividends."

"And fracking in a National Park will destroy the ability of future generations to enjoy our natural heritage."

"Future generations?" Dad seethed. "Where the fuck did that come from? If you cared about future generations you would have given me grandchildren."

Madison held on to a shred of unruffled composure, but just barely.

He shook his head. "You sound like a tree hugging nutjob."

Far from it, but not as far as she had been six months ago. "There are other ways to earn profits to pay shareholders, Dad."

"Such as?"

"Renewables."

"What?" He approached. "Now you've really gone off the deep end. Where'd my daughter go?" He knocked on her head.

She slapped his hand away. She stepped back, out of reach, trying to calm the ire now at a boiling point.

"I don't know who's been brainwashing you. Probably one of your loony feminist friends." He strolled back to stand behind his desk, his position of power.

"I'm being serious. Trust me, Dad, our turnaround will be good for business. Renewables are the wave of the future. It will bring new prestige to the Danes name."

"Oh no it will not. I won't give you a chance. I'm firing you. As of right this moment—" he punctuated each word with a thump on his desk, "you no longer work for Danergy."

Anger drowned the panic welling in her gut. "You can't do that without board approval."

"Oh, yes I can. Check your contract. I'll have Darleen send you the latest version."

Shit. Then what those guys in the bar at Mariano's had said was true. "You never trusted me. You never wanted me to be the CEO I was born to be."

"You were born to be a Hollywood wife and look how well that turned out."

Madison fought back tears of rage. Emotion would just feed into Dad's agenda.

"You'll get a letter from the board by the end of business. I suggest you to spend the rest of your day here clearing out your office."

"Luckily, I already have a plan to move forward. Leave Danergy in the dust." She'd have to pivot quickly to put her idea in motion.

He grunted. "And I will do everything in my power to crush that fucking bill in the House."

Madison turned on her high heels and stormed out of the office.

Fort America

"BOSS, I THINK you need to hear this."

Kace looked up from his paperwork. Paris stared at her phone as she leaned against his office door jamb.

"Oh, wow," she said, riveted to the glowing screen.

He stood. "Oh, wow, what, Paris?"

She looked up, dazed. "Sorry." She turned her attention back to her phone. "Headline news. Well, domestic news, anyway."

"You know you're not supposed to be reading the news during work time." A brand new federal employee rule prohibited discussing politics in the workplace. And the news these days was nothing but politics.

The directive had come down because resistance, such as the Rogues' alternate public servant social media accounts, continued to irritate the current administration.

Paris cleared her throat. "*A new bill to protect Fort America from energy development has been submitted to the House of Representatives by California Congresswoman Wendy Morton.*"

Okay. That got his full attention. "What?"

"That's what I thought," she said raising her eyebrows at him. "It gets better. *A separate bill allowing hydraulic fracturing— known commonly as fracking—at Fort America has passed the Senate, but is currently stalled in the House. Language in the new House bill, H.R.7402, negates the text of the earlier bill, S.3806.*"

"Yeah, 'oh wow' is right." He leaned against his desk and crossed his arms over his chest.

Paris chewed on her lower lip while continuing to read in silence. She inhaled dramatically as if readying herself for a performance. "*Ms. Morton cited evidence of an historic escaped slave presence*—I hate it when they use 'an' instead of 'a' before historic—*as a reason for the new bill. 'The intersection of African-American history, Native-American history, and the history of American women is a touchstone for history in the American Southwest,' she said.*" Paris rolled her eyes. "Okay, whatever. I guess I should be happy a Republican is using the term 'intersection' in her official statements."

"Paris," Kace said with a smile, "we won."

"Only sort of, boss. It's not a done deal."

No, it wasn't. And he really shouldn't get ahead of himself. But, well, he got his job back and was swimming in optimism.

"*Ms. Morton has gathered supporters for the bill from both sides of the aisle,*" Paris continued. "'*We intend to fast track passage,' she said. 'The expected passage of H.R.7402 will send a clear message that our National Parks are sacred.*'"

Perhaps his optimism was not misplaced.

"Oh, jeez, here's a doozy." Paris's eyes widened.

Kace straightened.

"*Ousted Danergy CEO Madison Danes has said she fully supports the House bill and will lobby for its passage.*"

"Ousted?"

"Yeah, ousted." Paris scrunched her brow. "Let me look that up."

Paris's index finger flew over her smart phone faster than Kace could type on a desktop keyboard with two hands.

"Okay, so, it says here *Madison Danes, daughter of Danergy founder Duke Danes, was fired from her position as Danergy CEO due to a conflict of core values.* Core values? What does that even mean?"

Kace had an inkling.

"There's a photo of her all dolled up." There was a brief pause before the cat-call. "Ooh-eeh, she doesn't look too shaken up by losing her job."

He ignored that, and, instead, imagined what Madison looked like the last time her saw her. Naked in his bed.

Nope. Should not think about such things at work. Worse than politics.

"Looks like she's got something else up her sleeve," continued Paris. "*Ms. Danes is concentrating her efforts on managing her Dama Energy Foundation, a non-profit helping women achieve success in energy and engineering-related careers.* So there you go. That's what Ms. Tight Jeans—" Paris glanced back at her phone "—or, rather, Ms. Short Skirt is doing these days."

He puffed out a breath. "Wow."

"You didn't know any of this?"

"No, not at all."

"So you and Madison don't keep in touch?"

"Not really." Their connection was more like a series of booty calls with dinner. Not a relationship.

Paris smiled. "Looks like she's on our side now."

"Yeah, I guess it does." Kace's heart thumped as optimism turned to excitement.

CHAPTER FOURTEEN

Washington, D.C.

Madison lay in bed in her usual five-star D.C. hotel room. Her head buzzed, refusing to let her body slip into that first plane of relaxation before drowsiness. She turned on her side and hugged the pillow more closely, hoping sleep would come in a new position. Instead, she was greeted with the digital clock on the nightstand announcing it was three in the morning.

Fuck.

She'd had a long day of lobbying on Capitol Hill. A very long day. And more to come.

The vote on H.R.7402 was in two days. She desperately needed to get some sleep. Instead, her brain decided the middle of the night was the best time to run through every little thing she had said to every representative.

Exhaustion overwhelmed her, but her eyelids refused to cooperate.

Her phone buzzed. Who the fuck calls someone at three a.m.?

A split second of wishful hope for Kace was shattered when the photo of Congressman Jim Lessing illuminated the screen.

If she weren't so fucking desperate to pass the legislation, she'd let this one go. Jim was a political crony of Dad's and usually favorable to Danergy. She needed his support.

"Hello, Jim."

"Madison? Sorry to wake you."

"I couldn't sleep, anyway. I'm up early."

"I hear you. I just got to the office—"

Some representatives worked a little too hard.

"And saw you'd left a message last night. What's this about?"

"House bill 7402."

He snorted a laugh. "I got an earful from your father yesterday."

She'd thought as much. "I'm not working with my father on this one, Jim. In fact, I'm working against him."

A blip of silence was followed by an "Oh? Yeah, I guess I heard about your split."

"I want you to vote yes on the bill."

"Okay." The lilt in his response made him sound intrigued at least. "Give me your pitch."

Spoken like a true businessman. You could put a businessman in Congress but you'd never truly change him into an impartial public servant.

Her pitch would have to be unique to get Jim's attention. He was one of the key votes in this. He had a lot of respect among conservatives.

Madison silently inhaled courage.

"During the Gulf War, an American soldier went to Iraq. Not to fight, though, although he did see his fair share of injuries and deaths. He went to Iraq to save, to protect, to preserve. His mission was to safeguard Iraq's ancient heritage from the kind of exploitation that happens in times of chaos. He carefully unearthed and cataloged ancient artifacts after bombings and destruction, saving them from the black market. He helped protect museum collections from dispersal to collectors who had no interest in the people of Iraq, but were only interested in their own avariciousness. His goal was to save Iraqi culture for the Iraqi people.

"He was as successful as a small group of soldiers could be in a time of war.

"When he returned to the United States he made it his mission to do the same for American culture. Preserving what he could, teaching others about its importance, saving it from destruction.

"He was successful. Until today.

"Now there are forces that seek to destroy what this war veteran has spent decades protecting. But this is not an enemy. It's friendly fire. And he's losing.

"I want to help him preserve American heritage for all Americans. Not destroy American heritage for a small group of profit-seekers."

Jim blew out a sigh. "You're talking about that National Park ranger at the Senate energy committee hearing."

"Yes. Kace Jaager, the superintendent of Fort America."

"I remember him. In your story he comes off as one of those World War Two Monuments Men saving European treasures from Hitler."

"He was. Except it was cuneiform tablets and other ancient artifacts in Iraq."

Another sigh. "Madison, the Senate bill is about energy self-sufficiency, so we don't have to fight wars in the Middle East anymore. The co-sponsors of the new bill need to understand that."

"But there are other ways to achieve that goal."

"Okay, I'll bite. Such as?"

"Renewables. Solar, geothermal, wind energy, tidal power."

He laughed. "You sound like a radical, not the daughter of Duke Danes."

"With all due respect congressman, the time has come for the old guard to reevaluate their business practices. If all the oil in private land has dried up, we can't start destroying our own heritage for a few more gallons. We have to rethink our entire energy policy. And businesses have to start investing in other forms of energy production."

The silence at the other end of the line lasted a little too long for comfort. "Let me think about this. I got a lot of oil industry folk breathing down my neck."

"You also have a nascent solar panel industry in your state."

"Yes, yes, I do." He grunted. "I guess I'll see you in the next couple of days?"

"I got to get away, Jim. Take in some fresh air and beautiful scenery while we still have it."

A grim chuckle. "Good night, Madison."

She ended the call and rolled onto her back. Now that she had done all she could, getting the hell out of dodge sounded like a great idea.

Fort America

"*WITH THE VOTE on House bill 7402 today, environmentalists across the United States are on stand-by. With Republicans in control of the House, will it be a win or a loss for America's National Parks?*"

Kace paused from straightening up the shelves of historic photo-filled books on Fort America. "Paris, you know you're not supposed to read news on work time."

"Yeah, yeah," she said, not looking up from her phone.

Well, it *was* before ten in the morning when the visitor center opened to the public, so no one was there to hear. Especially since they now knew the visitor center was not bugged.

Kace chuckled to himself. In a fit of angry paranoia after the no-politics-at-work dictum had gone down, Paris had done a bug sweep. Apparently she'd done similar tasks during her army days. She'd come up empty handed, to everyone's relief.

The morning after, Paris had argued convincingly that it was important for the staff and volunteers to be apprised of current events, especially since Fort America's fate *was* a current event. She wired the interactive video display monitor to run C-SPAN, and, when nothing interesting was going on in Washington, she scanned news sites for relevant tidbits and read them out loud.

"Kace," Paris said, "you'll find this interesting."

He paused, fortifying himself against bad news.

"*Madison Danes, formerly CEO of Danergy, has issued a press release via her non-profit, the Dama Energy Foundation, supporting the legislation. She stated if the legislation passes she will be pursuing an array of energy projects.*" Paris laughed. "Array? Whoever writes Madison's press releases has a sense of humor."

"Thank you, Ms. Anderson. I write my own press releases."

Kace popped up at the sound of Madison's voice. She stood in the doorway in crumpled casual clothes, her lack of makeup exposing the bags under her eyes. Her blond hair was swept back in a loose pony tail. A long cylindrical container hung from a strap slung over her shoulder.

He swallowed. "Ms. Danes, you look—"

"Like you drove all night just to see us." Paris shot Kace a warning look.

Yeah. One should never tell a beautiful woman she looked tired. Plus, Paris's observation was perceptive. Madison did look like she'd been up all night.

"I'll admit I haven't had a solid night's sleep for a few days. I've been in D.C. lobbying for the passage of H.R.7402."

Kace froze in place. That was not what he was expecting. "You were fighting to pass the bill?"

"The vote's today," Paris said quietly.

"I am acutely aware of this." Madison swung the cylindrical container off her shoulder. "I've got something to show you." She tapped the top of the box as she addressed Kace. "Perhaps in your office?"

Kace gestured for her to lead the way. Once inside he closed the door behind them, then reopened it and left it ajar. A securely closed door would give his dick inappropriate ideas.

Madison seemed unaware of her disturbance to his libido. She moved efficiently to his desk, opened up the cylinder, and removed a set of blueprints. She unrolled them, smoothing them at the center.

"Remember when you told me one way for women to be in charge of energy in this country is to take charge of industries ignored by men?"

"I said that to you?"

"I think you were desperate to get me to leave the dark side."

He chuckled and stepped behind her, breathing in a clean scent unmasked by perfume.

"If the vote goes as hoped today, I have a new plan." There was a slight tremble to her voice.

"What do you mean?" He gently urged her to face him. "Madison, what's going on?"

"Dad fired me."

"I heard. So what really happened?"

She bit her lower lip, pale pink and bare of lipstick. "After our night together," she looked away as if afraid to meet his gaze, "I had an idea. A revelation, really. If Dad meant for me to be merely a figurehead, I would prove to him I was in fact in charge. I decided I would act with the full authority allotted to me as CEO."

She looked nothing like the CEO she had once been. She looked like a strong woman unfettered by expectations and opinions.

"I sent out an official press release as CEO saying Danergy was against fracking on public lands."

"Oh, wow."

She smiled at his reaction. "Dad was so effing mad, he fired me."

"Clearly, that did not stop you."

"No. I don't think I've ever been so determined in my life." She placed her hands on the blueprints. "I have this crazy idea to set up an alternative energy demonstration building near your park."

"What?" *the actual fuck?*

"I'm serious. Take a look."

Kace stared at the blueprints, focusing his glazed eyes on the details. Solar panels on the roof. A separate solar array alongside the building. Wind turbines. Geothermal. A rain water catchment system. Gray water recycling.

Shit. He gaped at her. "You're planning on building this?" *Wait.* He narrowed his eyes. "Where? On federal land? Is this some sort of compromise?"

"No," she yelped. She pursed her lips as she drew in a long inhalation. "No. Private land. Near Freegate." She met his gaze. "Land I purchased a while ago knowing I would have to live somewhere other than the hotel while overseeing the fracking operation."

"Huh." He resumed his perusal of the plans. "So tell me more about your idea."

"Well," she began, enthusiasm quickening her words, "it's going to be a non-profit educational facility operated by the Dama Energy Foundation to teach kids all about renewables." She pulled back the top page to reveal a site plan. "There's a campground here. I want to establish internships and summer programs for kids to learn about history and nature and alternative energy. Supplementing your programs at Fort America, of course. Just one more opportunity to learn while on their field trips away from the big city."

"You're really doing this for the kids?"

"And for Fort America." Her cheeks colored. "And for you."

"For me?"

"Kace, I can't get you out of my mind."

Blood pumped to his groin. This was neither the time nor place, but, *damn*, if he didn't want to bend her over his desk and have his way with her.

Instead, he danced his fingers along her palm. "I feel very much the same," he murmured. He pulled his hand away. "But I suspect there is just a bit more at play with this scheme than a lowly park ranger."

"You're not lowly! I seem to recall a meme saying you were the hero America needed."

He chuckled as he met her gaze. "You're really doing this to get back at your dad."

She straightened her back. "Yeah, okay, that. Plus make a name for myself."

"I thought you were already famous."

"I am, but as a movie star's ex-wife and an evil energy company executive. I need to pivot publicly and dramatically." She sobered, and clasped his hand. "I *am* really on your side, Kace. While I was in D.C., I did all I could. You have to believe me."

"I do believe you." He squeezed her hand, soft and warm in his own. "I'm just astonished by all of this. By your turnaround."

"Like I said, you've really affected me," she said under her breath. "But I'm worried about the vote today."

"Whatever happens, happens." He snorted in disgust. "I've become resigned to it all."

"Yeah, but if it doesn't pass maybe I can do more lobbying to stall any projects until there's a more favorable administration."

He smirked. "You sound like a politician."

"I'm a former CEO. Basically the same thing these days. But whatever happens, I'm determined to build my project. If there's fracking going on in Fort America, the public needs to know how dangerous it is and what the alternatives are."

Incredible. He could kiss her—

A knock on the door sent Kace stepping backward and releasing his hold on Madison.

Paris poked her head in. "The debate's winding up. Looks like roll call's going down soon, boss."

Madison and Kace exchanged knowing glances. *The vote.*

"Paris has C-SPAN set up on the monitor in the visitor center."

Madison tugged on her lower lip with her teeth. "I suppose we should watch?" She shot a worried glance in Paris' direction.

"We're not being bugged," Paris said, suppressing a grin. "If that's your concern."

Madison laughed. "Well, okay then. Let's watch C-SPAN."

They found perching spots in the visitor center near the now far more prominently positioned video monitor.

The speaker of the House called for an electronic vote to take place over fifteen minutes. Immediately, the on-screen display showed a dozen Yea votes were cast, plus a handful of Nays, while the digital clock counted down the seconds.

Watching four hundred and thirty-five legislators vote—or rather, slightly fewer than four hundred and thirty-five because some were absent for various reasons—was not a task to be undertaken lightly. With Madison at Kace's side, the usually staid C-SPAN was like watching a gossipy talk show. She provided running commentary as they viewed representatives mill about in front of the podium.

"I met that guy," she said, pointing. "He wears the same damn tie like every day." And another. "She's sharp. Someone to watch." Still, someone else. "Hard drinker, but, whoa, what an intellect." After some laughter. "Oh, god, get a haircut."

One would not be able to match the party affiliation of any legislator based on Madison's comments. Her assessments were equal opportunity observations.

"Dad always called the Democrats a lost cause. But once I started talking to them, I realized they were politicians just like the Republicans, and, as all politicians, are usually willing to negotiate. Although along a slightly different spectrum."

During the first ten minutes of voting, any representative could change his or her vote. After only a few minutes in, the Yeas and Nays were equal.

Kace's gut churned as suspense and dread ate at him.

"I need to catch up on some emails."

Madison offered a thin smile. "Yeah."

Once inside his office, Kace leaned against the closed door. He couldn't watch the train wreck about to take place. Not long ago, Bureau of Land Management lands, *public* lands, had been auctioned off to the highest bidder for energy development, including fracking. Soon one of the most destructive forms of oil extraction would begin near—too near—sensitive natural National Monuments like Arches and Canyonlands. Why the hell was Fort America going to be any different? Why was he special?

Maybe because undeveloped public lands were seen as expendable, but National Parks were sacred?

Maybe because some legislators were feeling the pressure of the upcoming November election, with its predicted "blue wave" unseating conservative representatives?

Maybe because his obscure and unknown park was a little less so now that the celebrity Madison Danes had become involved?

"Involved" didn't quite define it. She was integrated, intertwined with Fort America and his life. She'd changed since that day they first met. She'd gone from dismissing him out of hand to embracing his beliefs. All right, she hadn't become an off-the-grid farmer, but she'd definitely changed.

Because of their conversations?

Because of their intimacy?

Somehow, because of him.

He plopped down onto his chair. Before him were the blueprints, more evidence that Madison had changed because of him. He ran a finger across the drawings, humbled by her efforts.

She'd taken the time to understand his beliefs, explore their intimacy, had used her connections to get his job back, and now she was at his side fighting to protect everything he cared about.

And what the hell had he done for her?

Nothing but try to control her, and when he'd realized he could not, he'd lost every shred of self-restraint and acted out. His inability to subdue her stubborn independence brought out a vicious asshole from deep within.

And yet at this very moment, all he wanted was to feel her arms around him, hear her telling him everything would be fine. At every chaotic turn in his life over the last few months, she'd been able to do something to fix his predicament or soothe that beast within.

Most importantly, he'd let her. He'd given up his need for control because he'd also changed. He'd grown to respect and admire the strong, intelligent, independent woman she was.

And had grown to trust her.

He stared at his computer monitor. He wasn't going to get any work done in the next five minutes.

He just wanted to be with her no matter what happened.

MADISON LOOKED between C-SPAN on the monitor and the Twitter stream on her phone. Amazingly the Alt_FortAmerica Twitter account was live streaming the vote tally. It had to be someone in-house. But Paris was busy opening the visitor center and tending to the tourists that had arrived. Becky had her back to Madison. She seemed too mild mannered and retired to be the brains behind a rogue social media account. Not all the staff was present, though, including—

Kace?

Wow. Was Kace behind the Fort America Rogue Twitter account? Maybe he wasn't looking at emails at all but was frantically pounding out tweets on his keyboard, his expression maniacal, his perfect gray hair disheveled, his tie askew.

Madison tried not to laugh.

She quickly sobered when Kace appeared in the hallway to his office.

He looked a wreck, and not in a he'd-just-been-frantically-tweeting kind of way. More in a I'm-tired-of-this-bullshit kind of way.

"Is it over?"

She held out her hand. "No. But we're winning."

His wan expression brightened. "Really?" He went to her side and surreptitiously took her hand.

A few more tourists stepped through the now opened visitor center, some casting curious glances at the television. Kace snorted.

"Looks like we've garnered a bit of fame with this bill," he muttered. "We never get this many tourists at this hour of the morning."

One of the female tourists smiled their way, then did a double take and stared a little longer. She tugged on her companion's sleeve and whispered to him.

Madison shifted on her feet and returned her attention to the vote. So she'd been recognized. Good. Maybe word would filter back to Dad about how serious she was.

Kace exhaled heavily. "This is the longest fifteen minutes of my life."

"And you were in a war."

"Yeah," he scoffed. "But this battle's really getting to me."

"I guess once you saved a cuneiform tablet, you saved it. This must be like watching Congress vote on whether to smash all those artifacts to bits."

"Huh," he grunted with a crooked smile. "That's very astute of you."

She wrapped her arm around his waist. "Is a public display of affection allowed in the workplace?"

He draped his arm across her shoulders. "Right now it is."

From across the room, Paris grimaced and shook her head at them.

Kace chuckled. "After being humiliated live on television, getting fired, and navigating a federal employee gag order, I think I have no more fucks left to give."

Madison gave him a gentle squeeze.

The Speaker pounded the gavel announcing the voting had closed for H.R.7402.

Kace tensed, his face pale as he looked at the monitor.

"On this vote the Yeas are two hundred and forty five, the Nays are one hundred and eighty. The bill is passed."

Madison stared at the monitor, disbelieving. "We won."

Kace gaped.

"Jesus H. Christ, we won." Paris blushed and clamped her hand over her mouth.

They *had* won. And by not a slim margin. All that damn lobbying had paid off.

Kace's stiff stance relaxed. "Thank you, thank you, thank you," he murmured as he pulled Madison into an embrace.

His heart thumped excitedly under her ear. She blinked back tears as she looked up at him, her smile reflected in the joy twinkling in his eyes.

He leaned over her, moving closer until his lips hovered above hers.

"Here?" she asked, the heat of his breath burning her query, her desire for him dizzying her.

"Here." He pressed his lips to hers before opening his mouth, deepening the kiss as he enveloped her in his arms. Her initial surprise at his audacity dissipated under his determination. She melded against him, looping her arms around his neck.

Scattered applause and whistles were mingled with camera flashes.

Madison pulled back. "Looks like we've caused a sensation."

He grinned as he touched his forehead to hers. "It does."

"You really have no fucks left to give, do you?"

The grin waned slightly. "I have just won a major victory because of you, and am absolutely overwhelmed with gratitude." He gave a quick nod in the direction of the crowd. "I think they would understand. I hope my boss does."

"Madison! Madison!" came an enthusiastic squeal.

She turned to the crowd. "Yes?"

A pretty young woman stepped forward, a pink bandanna wrapped around her straight black hair. "Can I get a picture of you and your boyfriend?"

The color rose in Kace's clean-shaven cheeks.

Madison smiled at him. "What does my boyfriend think?"

There was that grin again. "Sure." He wrapped his arm around her shoulders as they posed for picture takers. "So I'm your boyfriend now?" he murmured.

"You better believe it. And definitely worth the fight."

CHAPTER FIFTEEN

Fort America, the following spring

Kace drove his new electric SUV along the gravel road from his house to Freegate. The vehicle did not handle the rugged roads as well as his trusty Jeep, but his rich girlfriend had bought it for him, and, well, whenever he went to visit her, he liked to show his appreciation.

He grinned. His girlfriend. Madison.

After the legislation had passed, he'd taken a few days of vacation and she'd stayed with him. They never left the house, and barely left the bedroom.

The morning he was expected back at work, he'd leaned against the kitchen counter, coffee cup in hand, staring at her all beautiful and disheveled, while she checked her email at the table.

"Too bad this is the end."

Her fingers flew over her phone. "Yeah. Looks like I gotta fly back to L.A."

He sipped his coffee. "I mean us. This."

That had got her attention. She placed her phone screen-side down on the table. "It doesn't have to be."

"Yes, it does. One of us has to give if we're gonna have a relationship. I'm not giving up my job to move to the big city, and I'm sure you can't give up your shopping and fine wines." He winked.

She scowled. "I don't have to give up anything."

"How do you mean?"

"I have the privilege of wealth. I can have anything I want shipped in."

He snorted. "You compromising? For a man? Doesn't that go against your feminist sensibilities?"

"No. I am forging my own path. You just happen to be on it."

That had made him chuckle.

"Besides, I want to be directly involved with my new center. Don't worry," she'd said with a sly smile. "I'll be here a lot."

Kace turned onto the chip-sealed highway headed to town. After that conversation— and a little nookie—Madison had gone back to L.A. and he'd resumed work as if he didn't have a famous girlfriend. Although her fame had rubbed off a bit onto him and Fort America increasing their visitor counts.

As planning for the center had begun, Madison had stayed at the Bailey, visiting him on the weekends. Then one day, a few weeks after construction on her project had started, she just...stayed.

As they had grown closer, he'd learned that it was best to simply let go and let her do her thing. And she did.

Besides taking over the closet in the spare-bedroom-slash-office, she set up her own home office in one corner. She rearranged some furniture in the living room, appropriated some drawers and shelves in the bathroom, and, well, moved in.

"I guess you're living here now?" He'd said one morning, watching mesmerized as she applied makeup which she had assured him was organic and cruelty free.

She'd given him a quick peck. "Do you mind?"

"Not really."

"Good," she'd said with a smile. "It's so much easier."

"And more fun."

Raucous bathroom counter sex had ensued after that, which pretty much sealed the deal of their living together.

Kace chuckled. It took a couple of movie nights to warm Paris to the idea. But once Madison's Hollywood roots came to the fore, the two women found common ground and got along famously.

He grinned as he slowed the SUV over a particularly bumpy patch of road. He grinned a lot these days. Despite the chaos living with a new girlfriend always engendered, he was more at peace in his mind and body and…

Heart.

The grin turned into a laugh. Yep, if he had to admit it, he was falling hard and fast in love. Joy—not just desire—burbled within every damn time he saw her.

As the energy center came into view. Kace swelled with pride. He slowed as he drove past the sign chiseled in local granite, the name always bringing a smile to his face.

The Liberty Gowdy Center for Energy and the Environment.

Bettina had been so happy when she'd heard. She had consulted with Madison about a permanent historical exhibit housed in the center's lobby to give background to the story of Ruth, Roland, and Liberty Gowdy. Another display encouraged tourists to visit Fort America.

Kace parked at the charging station next to Madison's car. He plugged in the SUV, and strode up the gravel path lined with native plants to the center's entrance.

The receptionist nodded in greeting and waved him through to Madison's office. He knocked softly before entering and closing the door, a blip of delight stretching the smile on his face.

Madison beamed and rose from her office chair. "To what do I owe the pleasure?"

He plopped down two insulated lunch bags on the conference table. "You left your lunch in the fridge."

"Oops." She offered a bashful expression before giving him a peck on the cheek. "Thanks for the special delivery. I'm starved."

"I figured as much."

She removed the contents of her bag and set them on the table. A sandwich wrapped in waxed cloth, fresh fruit in yogurt in a reusable container, fair trade chocolate for dessert.

Madison had taken on the task of packing their lunches, which meant Kace's was always very much the same as hers, just a little more of it. He grabbed his sandwich out of the bag. "What's new at the center?"

She nodded as she munched. "Looks like Teach for America will be adding us as a stop on their Fort America program."

"Awesome."

"It is. And in other news, Max sent me my L.A. mail. An actress friend of mine is getting married. In India."

Kace swallowed. "India?"

"Her mother is Indian."

"Ah." He took a bit of sandwich. Despite initial protestations, Kace had grown to like Madison's sometimes exotic choice of sandwiches. This one was cheese and chutney on ciabatta—with some expensive aged cheddar—and really, really good.

"She's marrying a rock star. They're both really cool, down to earth. You'd like them."

Mouth full, Kace offered a grunt of approval.

"So? You want to go?"

He stared at her blankly for a moment before it clicked. "To India?"

"Yeah."

"To a wedding?"

She laughed. "That's the idea."

Alarm skittered up the back of his neck. And must have registered on his face.

Her eyes widened. "What's wrong? I thought you said you have like months of vacation coming to you."

He laughed. "Not quite."

"You can't possibly be worried about leaving Fort America in the very capable hands of your trustworthy staff?"

"No. That's not what I'm worried about." Jeez, how should he say this? "I mean, a big trip, a wedding, it's kind of a statement of, well, you know…" He met her gaze. "Us."

"There *is* an 'us', right?"

"Of course there is." *Shit.* He'd just been skating along in his new blissed-out comfort zone. He should've realized she'd want to take the relationship to the next level. Not that he didn't want to. He'd just never bothered to take that next step.

She grinned. "Good. Then it's settled. I'm giving you fair warning in case your passport is not up to date."

"Okay." Kace reached into his bag for the yogurt. Next to the plastic container was a small, square velvety box. He took it out. "What's this?"

A slight blush colored her cheeks. "A present." She jerked her chin in his direction. "Open it."

He popped it open. Tucked inside a lining of blue satin was a ring, a thick, flat silver band engraved with a landscape, inlaid with polished wood hills and a river of blue-green gemstones. "This is amazing." He studied the landscape as closely as he could without his reading glasses. "That's the park…and the river." He looked at her, astounded. "That's Fort America."

She smiled, her lashes damp. And then realization dawned.

Giddiness swirled in his head in a dizzying frenzy. "Oh my god…Oh my god…Madison."

She took the ring and knelt before him. "Kace Jaager, will you do me the honor of being my husband?"

He held out his left hand, trembling to the beat of his frantic heart. "I will, Madison Danes. With pleasure."

The ring fit perfectly, the band a presence he'd never before felt, and had never imagined he would ever feel.

Tears smarted in his eyes. He pulled her onto his lap and kissed her. "What if I had eaten my lunch at work?"

She giggled, as she drew a finger along his jaw. "I purposely forgot mine. I knew you would be a gentleman and deliver it. Or, I'd get a very confused text."

Joy filled him to buoyancy, the weight of the ring—physical and emotional—tethering him to the present.

He kissed her again, the tender warmth of her lips spiking erotic need. Unwittingly, he let loose a growl.

Madison laughed. "Not here, Mr. Jaager." She pressed a finger to his lips. "Well, not right now, anyway. Later tonight." She gave him a peck. "At home."

Kace grinned. Home. *Their* home. The place they'd each fought so hard to protect.

More from Regina Kammer

Contemporary romance with a touch of history
Undamaged (Stories from the San Juan Islands)
Modern Shorts: A Contemporary Romance Collection
Resistance: A Common Elements Romance

Provocative historical romance
Victorian
The Pleasure Device (Harwell Heirs Book 1)
Disobedience By Design (Harwell Heirs Book 2)
Where Destiny Plays (Harwell Heirs Book 3)
The Westerman Affair (Art & Discipline Book 1)

American Revolution
The General's Wife: An American Revolutionary Tale
Winter Interlude: An American Revolutionary Novelette
On the Eighteenth of January, '78; or, A Night At Valley Forge

Ancient World
Hadrian and Sabina: A Love Story
Ancient Shorts: An Ancient World Romance Collection

About the Author

Regina Kammer is a librarian, an art historian, and an award-winning, international best-selling, multi-published writer of provocative historical romance and contemporary romance with a touch of history. Her short stories and novels make history sexier, whether the era is Roman, Byzantine, Viking, American Revolution, or Victorian. She's even sexed up contemporary settings, Steampunk, and Greco-Roman mythology. She has been published by Cleis Press, Go Deeper Press, Ellora's Cave, House of Erotica, Story Ink, Loose Id, The Naughty Literati, and her own imprint, Viridium Press. She began writing historical fiction with romantic elements during National Novel Writing Month 2006, switching to erotica when all her characters suddenly demanded to have sex.

Keep up with Regina
Check out her website: https://reginakammer.com/
Never miss a new release! Subscribe to *Kammerotica News*:
https://reginakammer.com/newsletter/

Historical erotic romance by Regina

Victorian
The Pleasure Device (Harwell Heirs Book 1)
Disobedience By Design (Harwell Heirs Book 2)
Where Destiny Plays (Harwell Heirs Book 3)
The Westerman Affair (Art & Discipline Book 1)
The Demonstration
The Invitation
Disputed Boundaries (Stories from the San Juan Islands)

American Revolution
The General's Wife: An American Revolutionary Tale
Winter Interlude: An American Revolutionary Novelette
On the Eighteenth of January, '78; or, A Night At Valley Forge

Ancient World
Hadrian and Sabina: A Love Story
Ancient Shorts: An Ancient World Romance Collection

Steampunk
One Cheek Or Two? (Ockham Steam-Works Laboratory Chronicles 1)
Delia's Heartthrob (Ockham Steam-Works Laboratory Chronicles 2)
Swing Follies (Ockham Steam-Works Laboratory Chronicles 3)